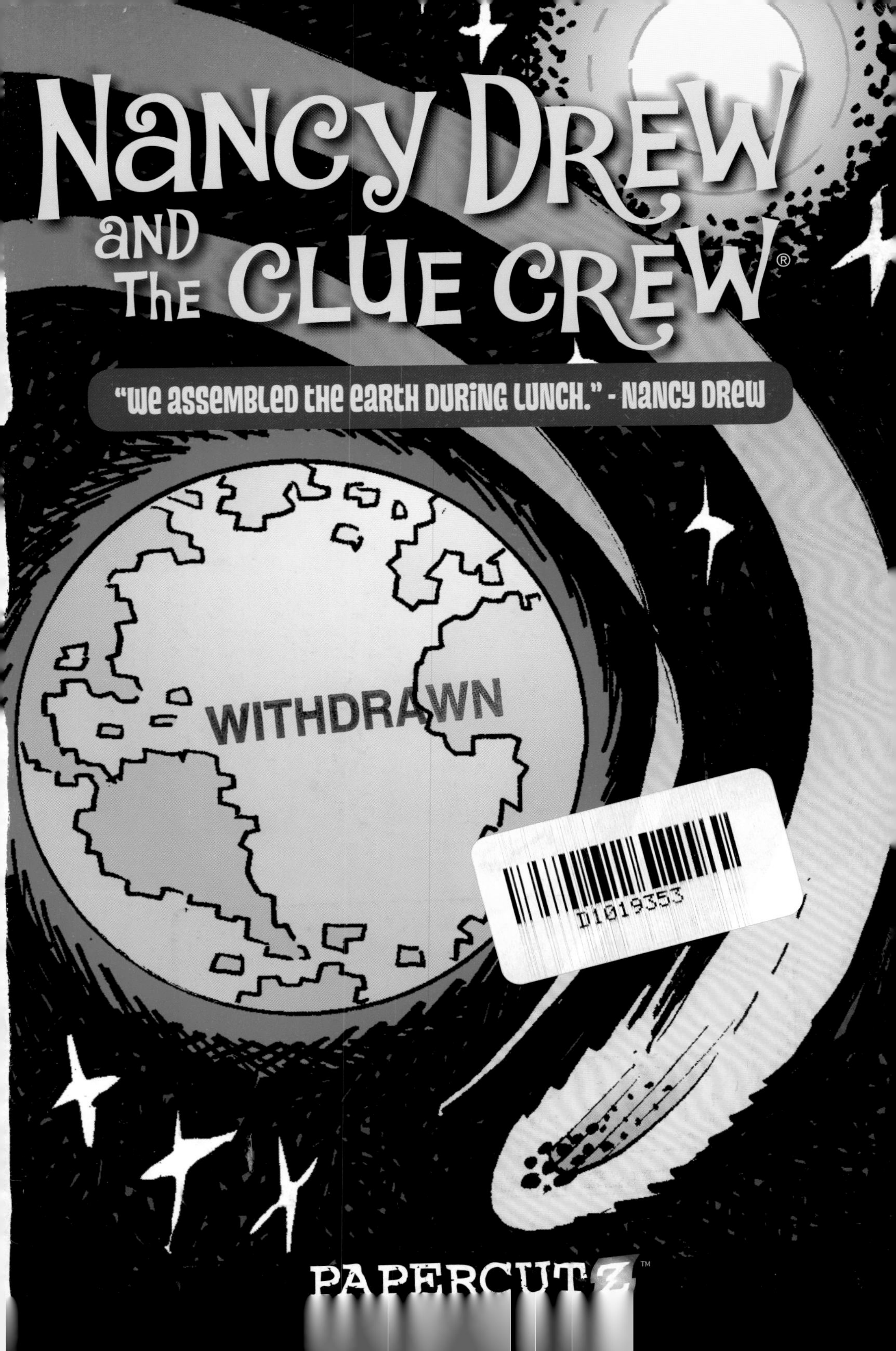
NANCY DREW
AND THE CLUE CREW®
"WE ASSEMBLED THE EARTH DURING LUNCH." - NANCY DREW
PAPERCUTZ™

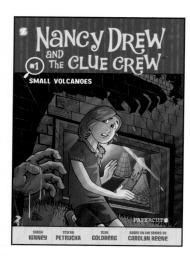

NANCY DREW
AND THE CLUE CREW
#1

SMALL VOLCANOES

SARAH KINNEY & STEFAN PETRUCHA - WRITERS

STAN GOLDBERG - ARTIST

LAURIE E. SMITH - COLORIST

BASED ON THE SERIES BY CAROLYN KEENE

PAPERCUTZ™
NEW YORK

For Maia & Margo
– SK & SP

For my granddaughter,
Bridget Hallie Doyle Goldberg
– SG

Nancy Drew and the Clue Crew
#1 "Small Volcanoes"
Sarah Kinney & Stefan Petrucha – Writers
Stan Goldberg – Artist
Laurie E. Smith – Colorist
Tom Orzechowski – Letterer
Production by Nelson Design Group, LLC
Associate Editor – Michael Petranek
Jim Salicrup
Editor-in-Chief

ISBN: 978-1-59707-354-7 paperback edition
ISBN: 978-1-59707-355-4 hardcover edition

Printed in China
August 2012 by Asia One Printing, LTD
13/F Asia One Tower
8 Fung Yip St., Chaiwan, Hong Kong

Distributed by Macmillan

First Printing

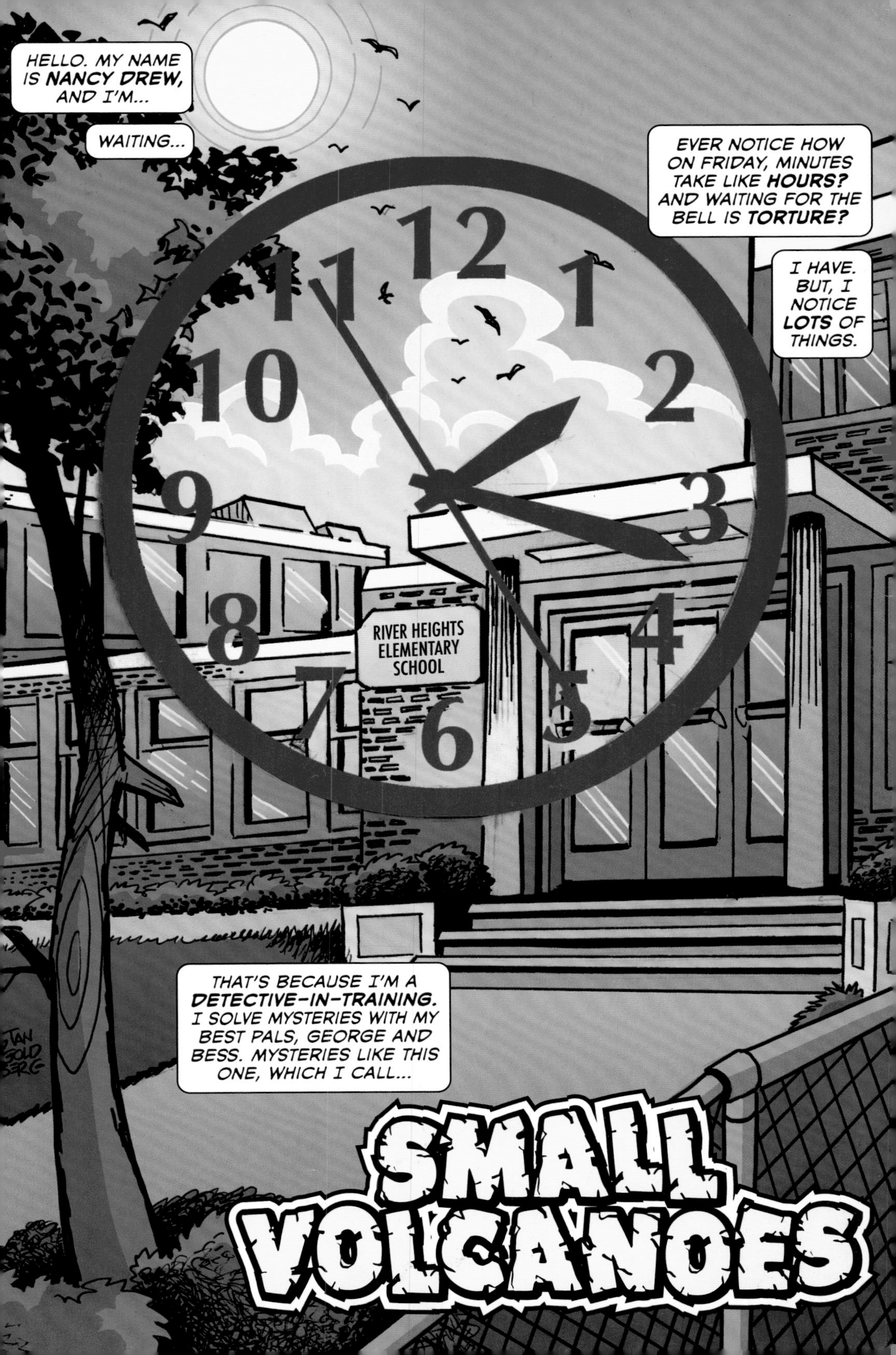
HELLO. MY NAME IS NANCY DREW, AND I'M...
WAITING...
EVER NOTICE HOW ON FRIDAY, MINUTES TAKE LIKE HOURS? AND WAITING FOR THE BELL IS TORTURE?
I HAVE. BUT, I NOTICE LOTS OF THINGS.
RIVER HEIGHTS ELEMENTARY SCHOOL
THAT'S BECAUSE I'M A DETECTIVE-IN-TRAINING. I SOLVE MYSTERIES WITH MY BEST PALS, GEORGE AND BESS. MYSTERIES LIKE THIS ONE, WHICH I CALL...
STAN GOLDBERG
SMALL VOLCANOES

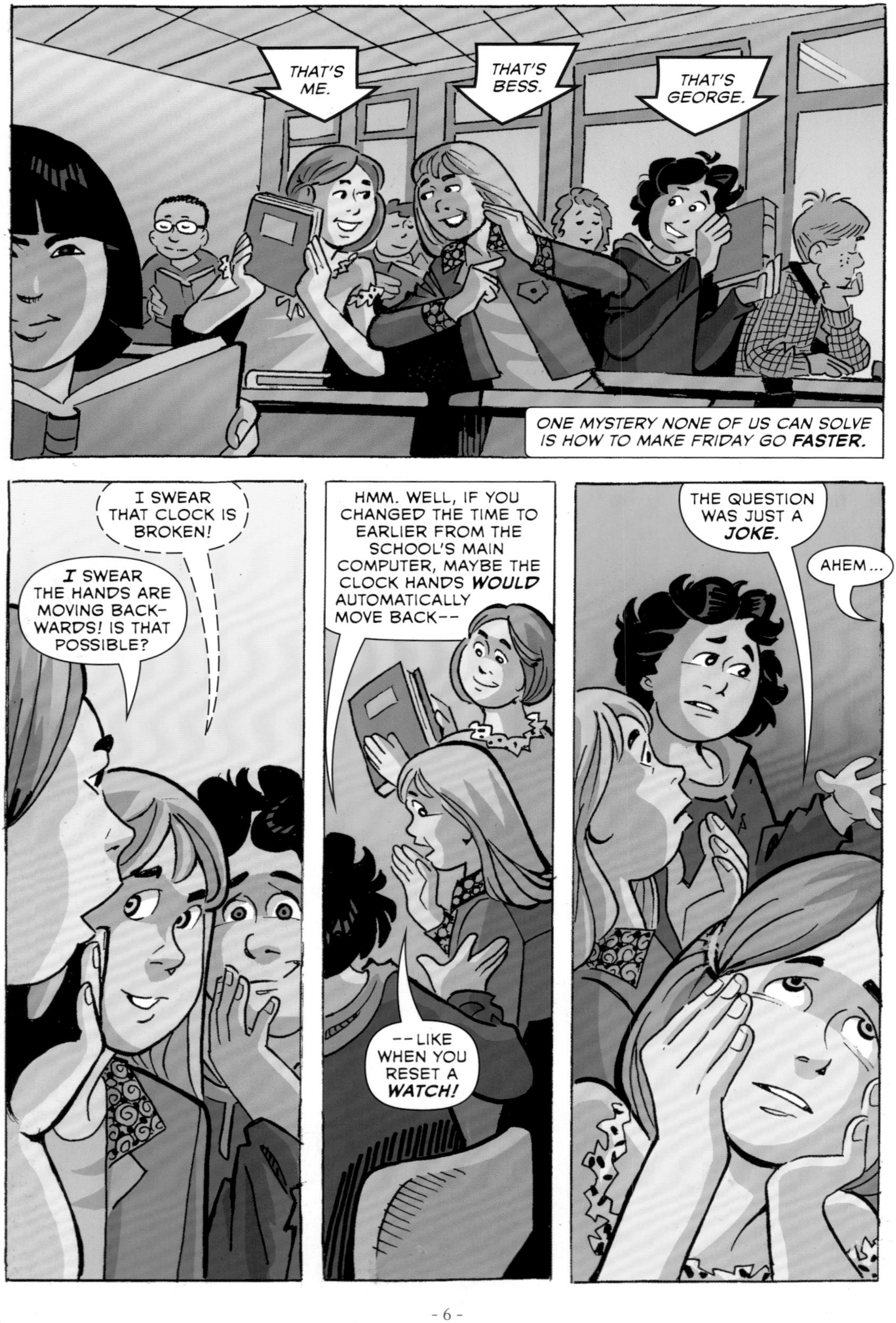
THAT'S ME.
THAT'S BESS.
THAT'S GEORGE.
ONE MYSTERY NONE OF US CAN SOLVE IS HOW TO MAKE FRIDAY GO **FASTER.**
I SWEAR THAT CLOCK IS BROKEN!
I SWEAR THE HANDS ARE MOVING BACK-WARDS! IS THAT POSSIBLE?
HMM. WELL, IF YOU CHANGED THE TIME TO EARLIER FROM THE SCHOOL'S MAIN COMPUTER, MAYBE THE CLOCK HANDS ***WOULD*** AUTOMATICALLY MOVE BACK--
--LIKE WHEN YOU RESET A ***WATCH!***
THE QUESTION WAS JUST A ***JOKE.***
AHEM...

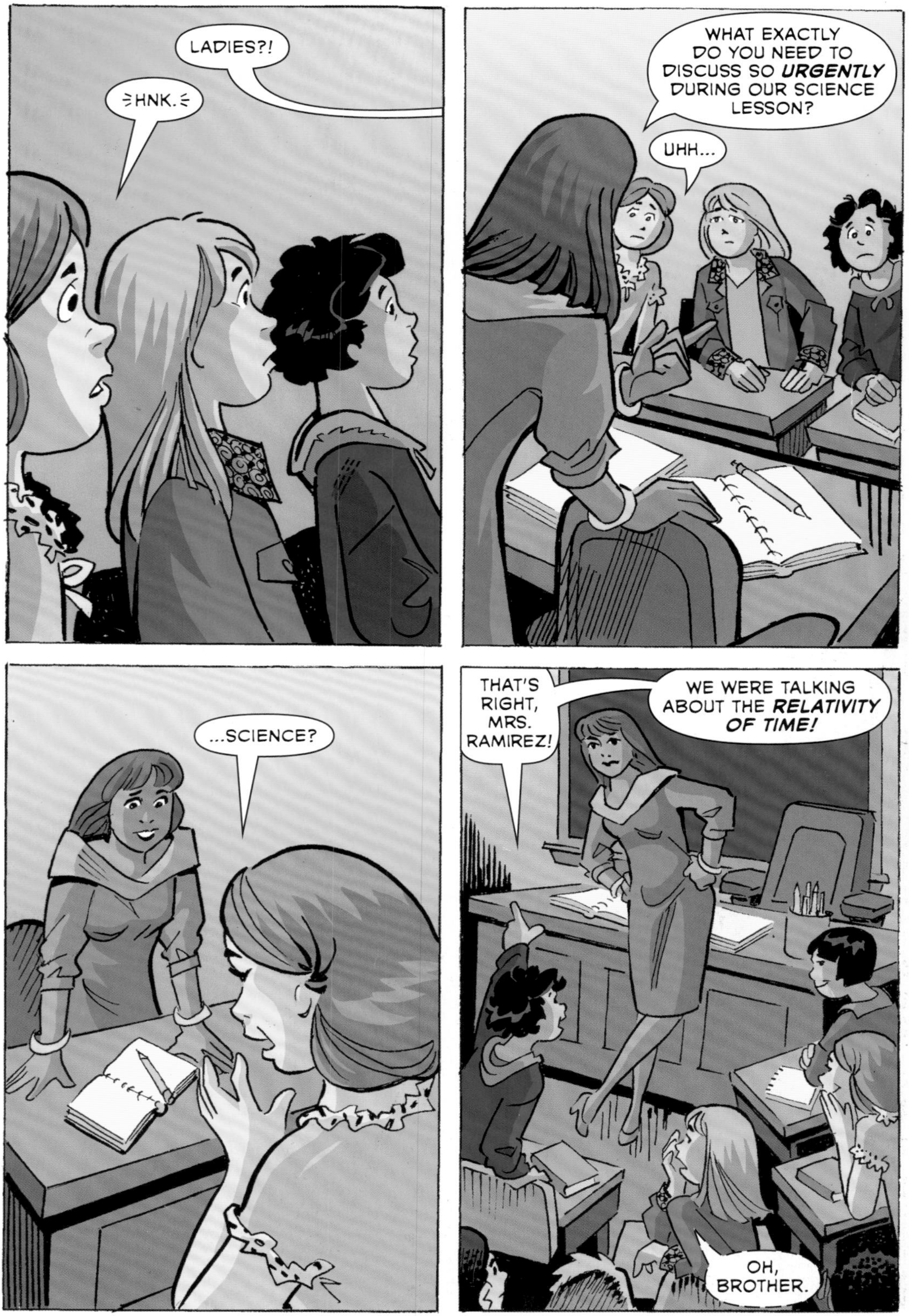

LADIES?!
HNK.
WHAT EXACTLY DO YOU NEED TO DISCUSS SO URGENTLY DURING OUR SCIENCE LESSON?
UHH...
...SCIENCE?
THAT'S RIGHT, MRS. RAMIREZ!
WE WERE TALKING ABOUT THE RELATIVITY OF TIME!
OH, BROTHER.

WELL, JUST MAKE SURE TO **MAKE TIME** THIS WEEKEND TO COME UP WITH IDEAS. IF YOU PLAN TO WORK AS A TEAM, THE PROJECT HAD BETTER BE A DARN GOOD ONE.

All science project ideas must be handed in on Monday!

LIKE A VOLCANO!

All science project ideas must be handed in

THAT'S FINE, BRIAN, BUT PLEASE DON'T CALL OUT.

YOU CAN WORK IN TEAMS OF UP TO **THREE,** BUT IF YOU **DO,** PLEASE KNOW THAT I EXPECT AN **EXCEPTIONAL** PROJECT.

ALL RIGHT!

NO PROBLEM FOR AN EXCEPTIONAL TEAM!

LIKE US!

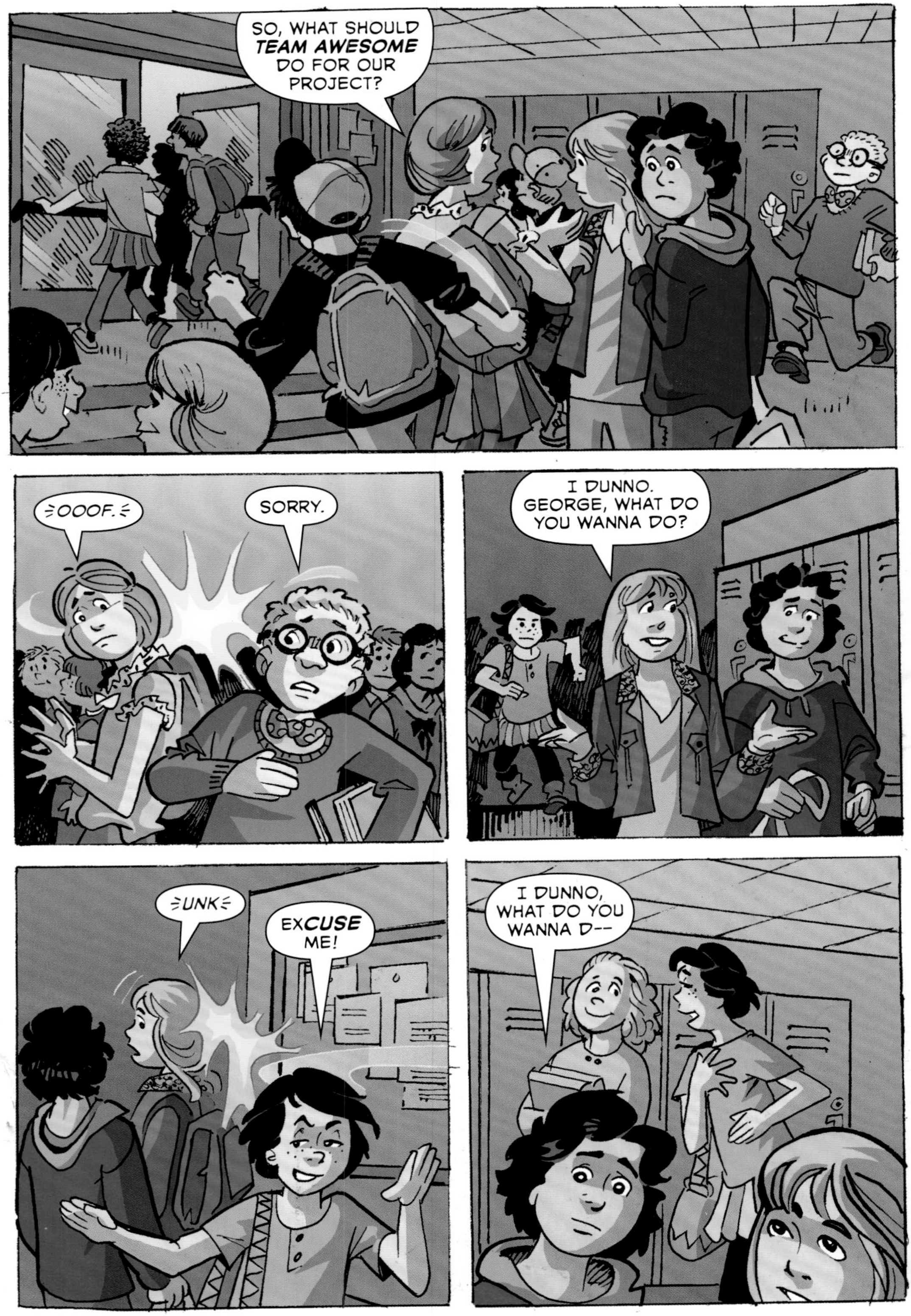
SO, WHAT SHOULD *TEAM AWESOME* DO FOR OUR PROJECT?
OOOF.
SORRY.
I DUNNO. GEORGE, WHAT DO YOU WANNA DO?
UNK
EX*CUSE* ME!
I DUNNO, WHAT DO YOU WANNA D--

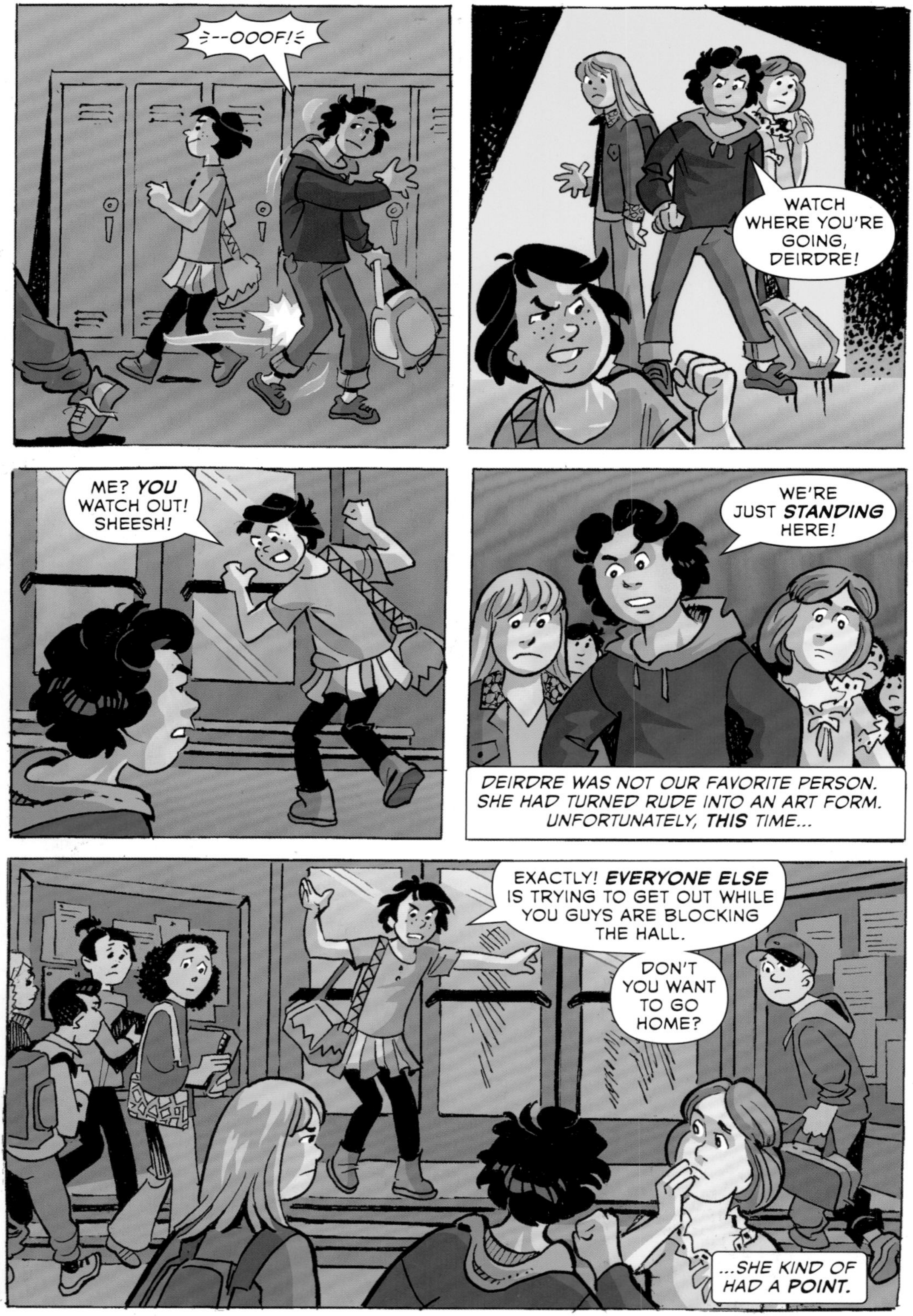
--OOOF!
WATCH WHERE YOU'RE GOING, DEIRDRE!
ME? YOU WATCH OUT! SHEESH!
WE'RE JUST STANDING HERE!
DEIRDRE WAS NOT OUR FAVORITE PERSON. SHE HAD TURNED RUDE INTO AN ART FORM. UNFORTUNATELY, THIS TIME...
EXACTLY! EVERYONE ELSE IS TRYING TO GET OUT WHILE YOU GUYS ARE BLOCKING THE HALL.
DON'T YOU WANT TO GO HOME?
...SHE KIND OF HAD A POINT.

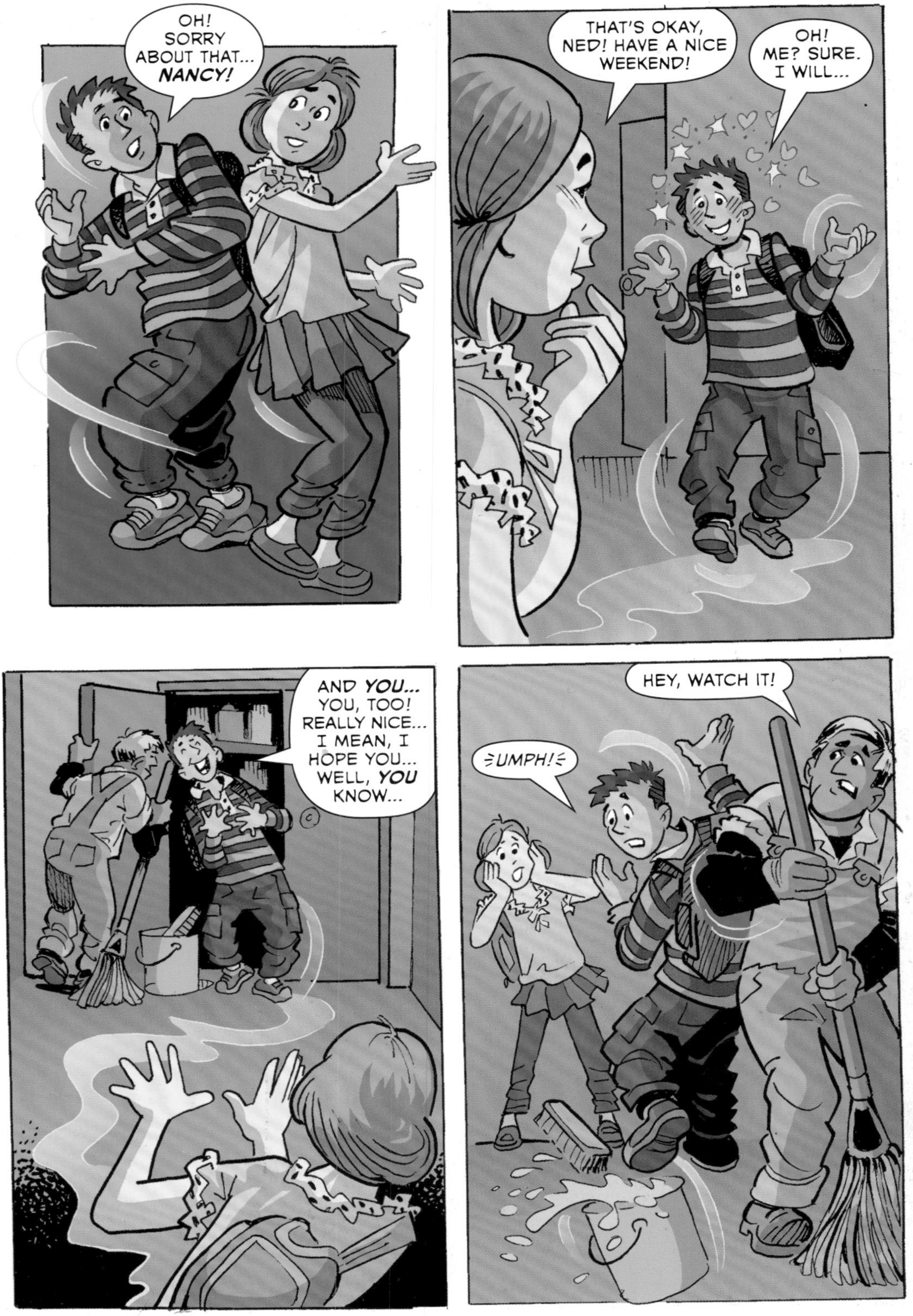
OH! SORRY ABOUT THAT... NANCY!
THAT'S OKAY, NED! HAVE A NICE WEEKEND!
OH! ME? SURE. I WILL...
AND YOU... YOU, TOO! REALLY NICE... I MEAN, I HOPE YOU... WELL, YOU KNOW...
HEY, WATCH IT!
UMPH!

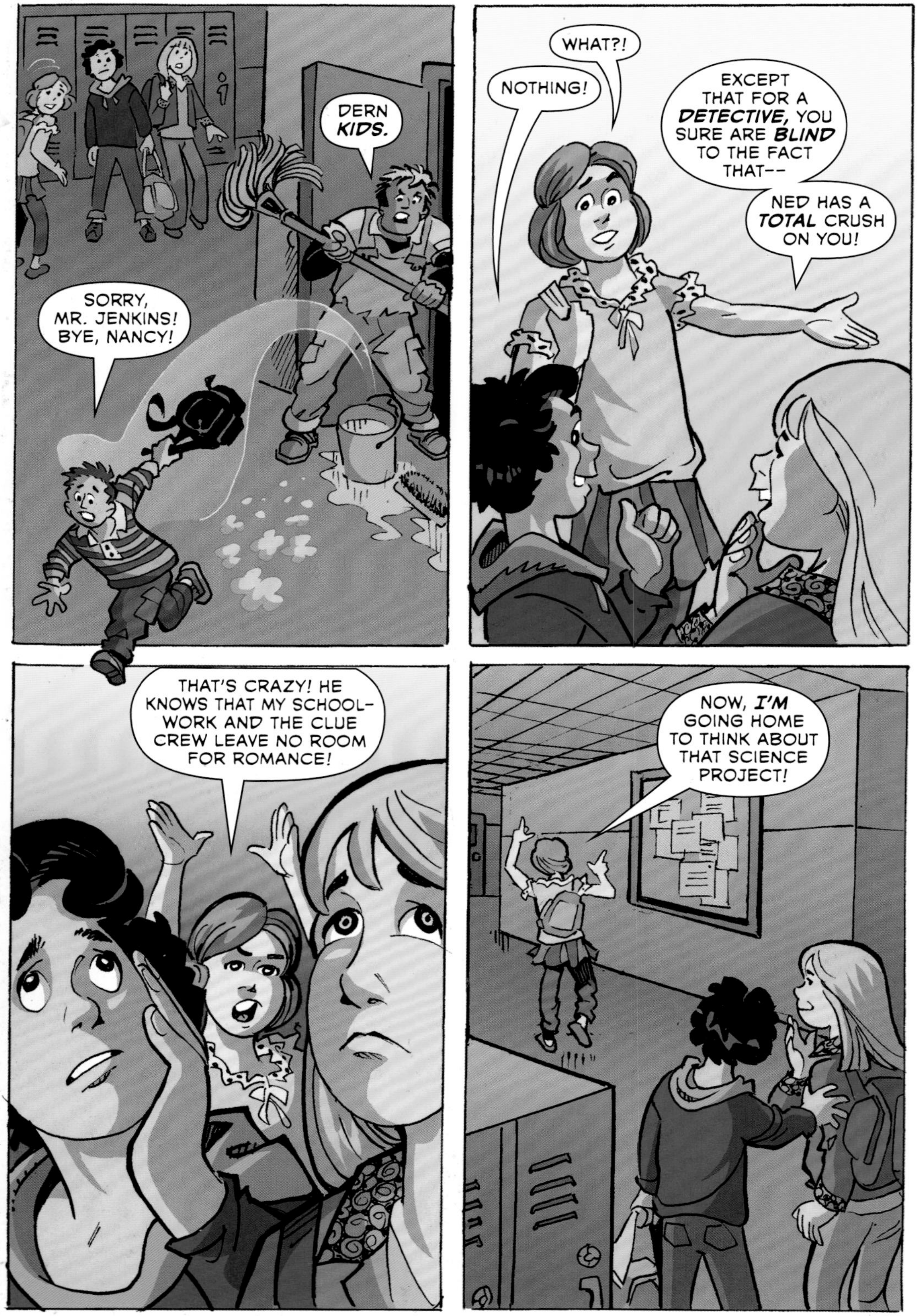
DERN KIDS.
SORRY, MR. JENKINS! BYE, NANCY!
WHAT?!
NOTHING!
EXCEPT THAT FOR A DETECTIVE, YOU SURE ARE BLIND TO THE FACT THAT--
NED HAS A TOTAL CRUSH ON YOU!
THAT'S CRAZY! HE KNOWS THAT MY SCHOOL-WORK AND THE CLUE CREW LEAVE NO ROOM FOR ROMANCE!
NOW, I'M GOING HOME TO THINK ABOUT THAT SCIENCE PROJECT!

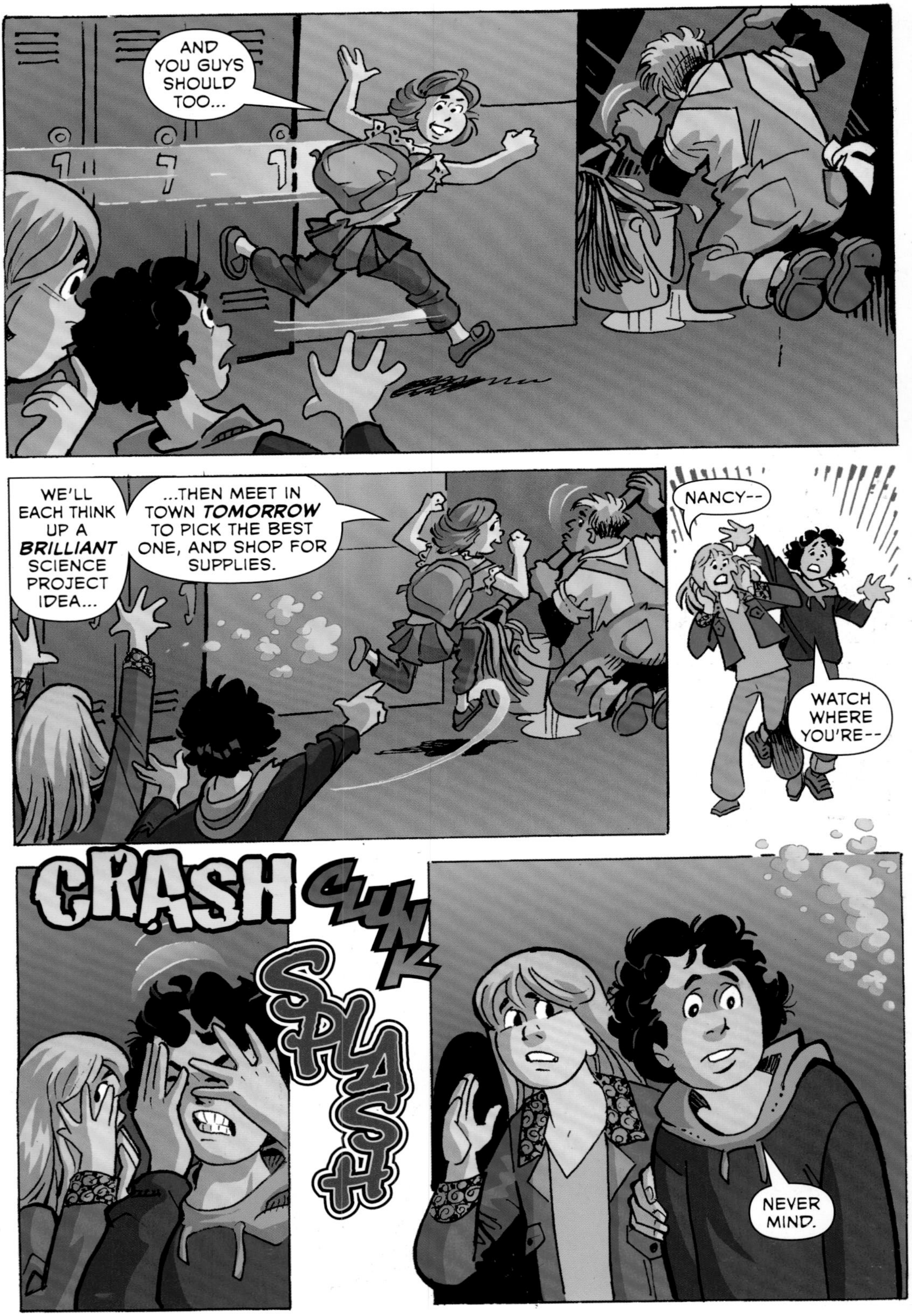
AND YOU GUYS SHOULD TOO...
WE'LL EACH THINK UP A BRILLIANT SCIENCE PROJECT IDEA...
...THEN MEET IN TOWN TOMORROW TO PICK THE BEST ONE, AND SHOP FOR SUPPLIES.
NANCY--
WATCH WHERE YOU'RE--
CRASH
CLUNK
SPLASH
NEVER MIND.

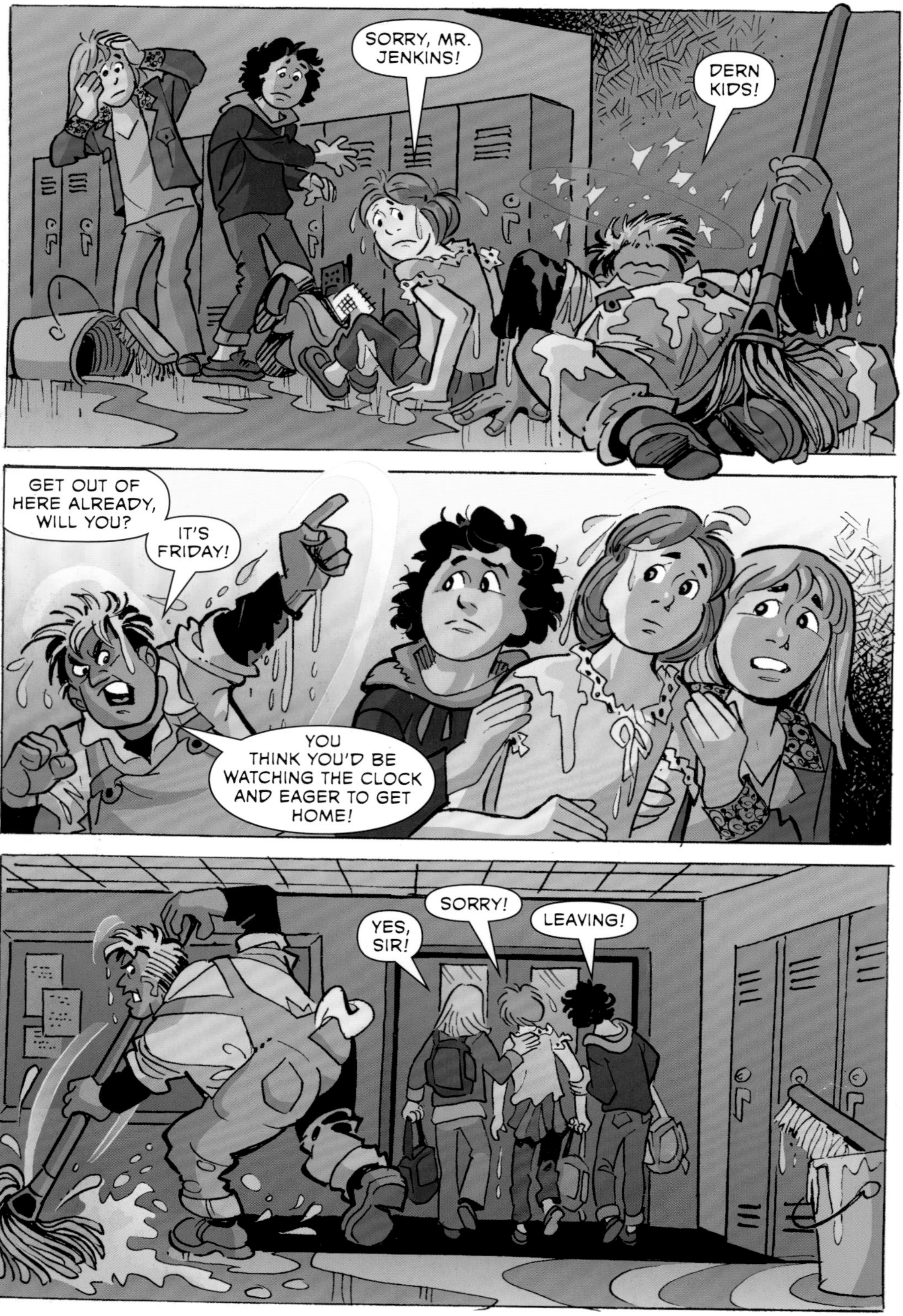
SORRY, MR. JENKINS!
DERN KIDS!
GET OUT OF HERE ALREADY, WILL YOU?
IT'S FRIDAY!
YOU THINK YOU'D BE WATCHING THE CLOCK AND EAGER TO GET HOME!
YES, SIR!
SORRY!
LEAVING!

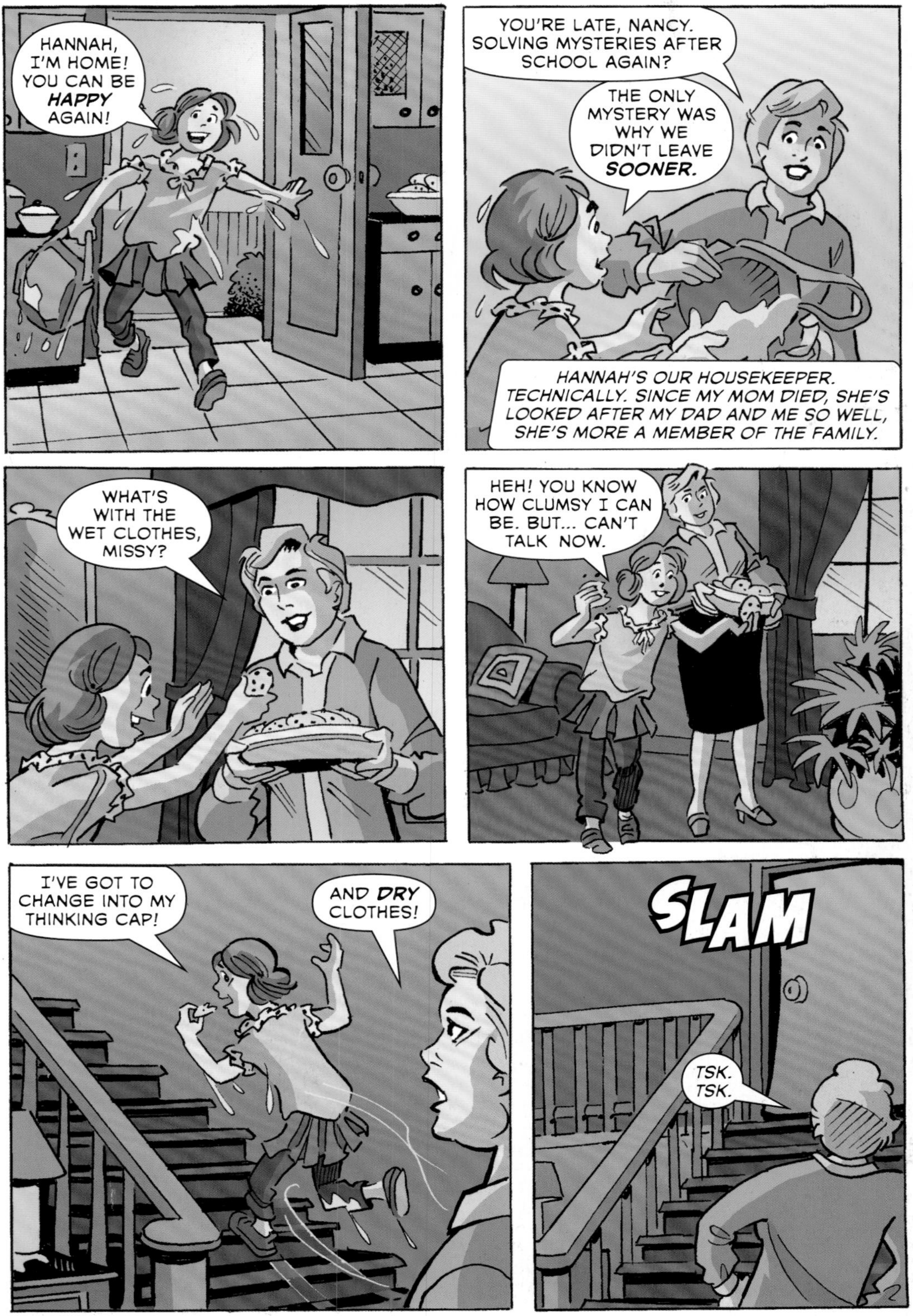
HANNAH, I'M HOME! YOU CAN BE *HAPPY* AGAIN!
YOU'RE LATE, NANCY. SOLVING MYSTERIES AFTER SCHOOL AGAIN?
THE ONLY MYSTERY WAS WHY WE DIDN'T LEAVE *SOONER.*
HANNAH'S OUR HOUSEKEEPER. TECHNICALLY. SINCE MY MOM DIED, SHE'S LOOKED AFTER MY DAD AND ME SO WELL, SHE'S MORE A MEMBER OF THE FAMILY.
WHAT'S WITH THE WET CLOTHES, MISSY?
HEH! YOU KNOW HOW CLUMSY I CAN BE. BUT... CAN'T TALK NOW.
I'VE GOT TO CHANGE INTO MY THINKING CAP!
AND *DRY* CLOTHES!
SLAM
TSK. TSK.

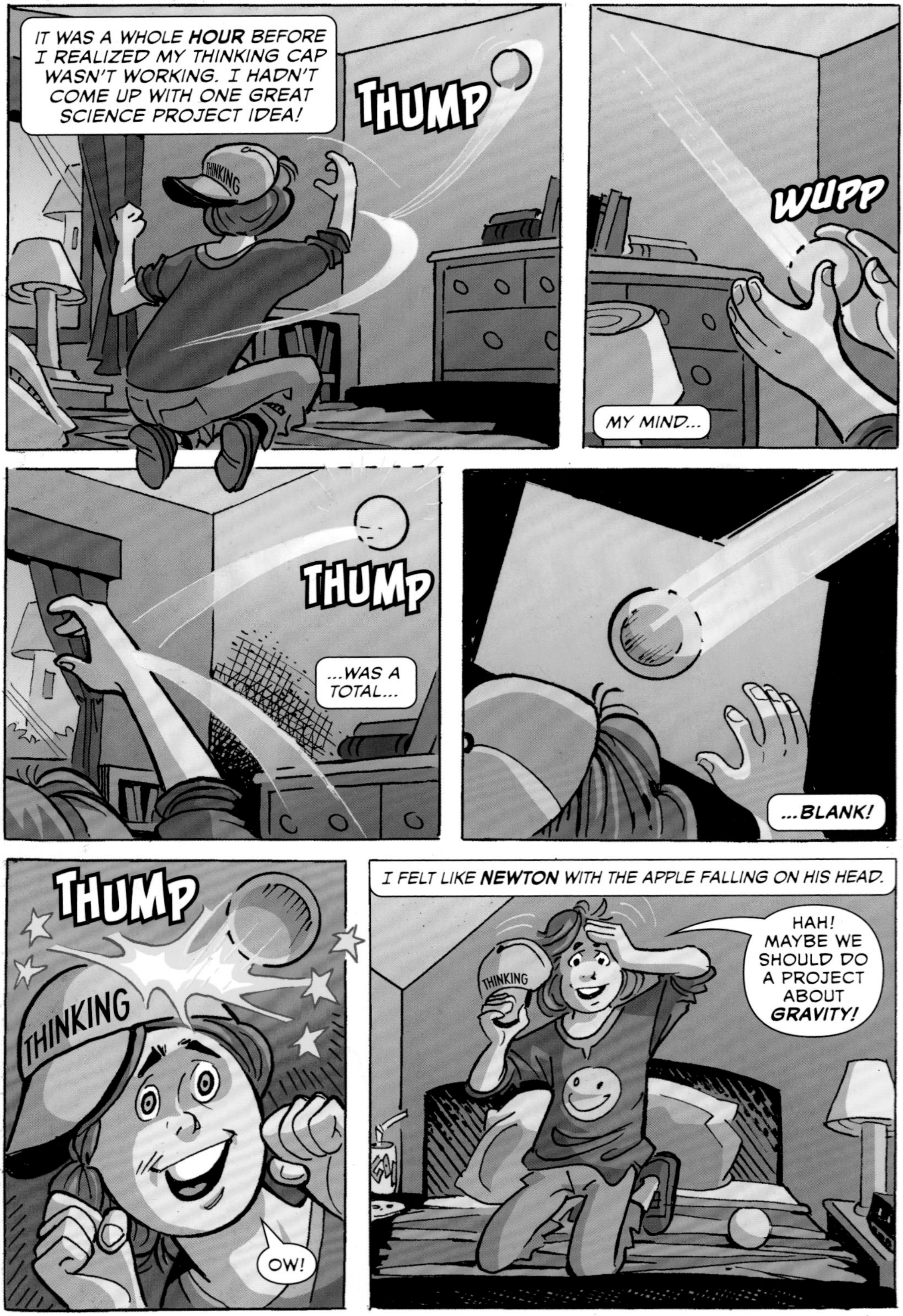
IT WAS A WHOLE HOUR BEFORE I REALIZED MY THINKING CAP WASN'T WORKING. I HADN'T COME UP WITH ONE GREAT SCIENCE PROJECT IDEA!
THUMP
THINKING
WUPP
MY MIND...
THUMP
...WAS A TOTAL...
...BLANK!
THUMP
THINKING
OW!
I FELT LIKE NEWTON WITH THE APPLE FALLING ON HIS HEAD.
HAH! MAYBE WE SHOULD DO A PROJECT ABOUT GRAVITY!
THINKING

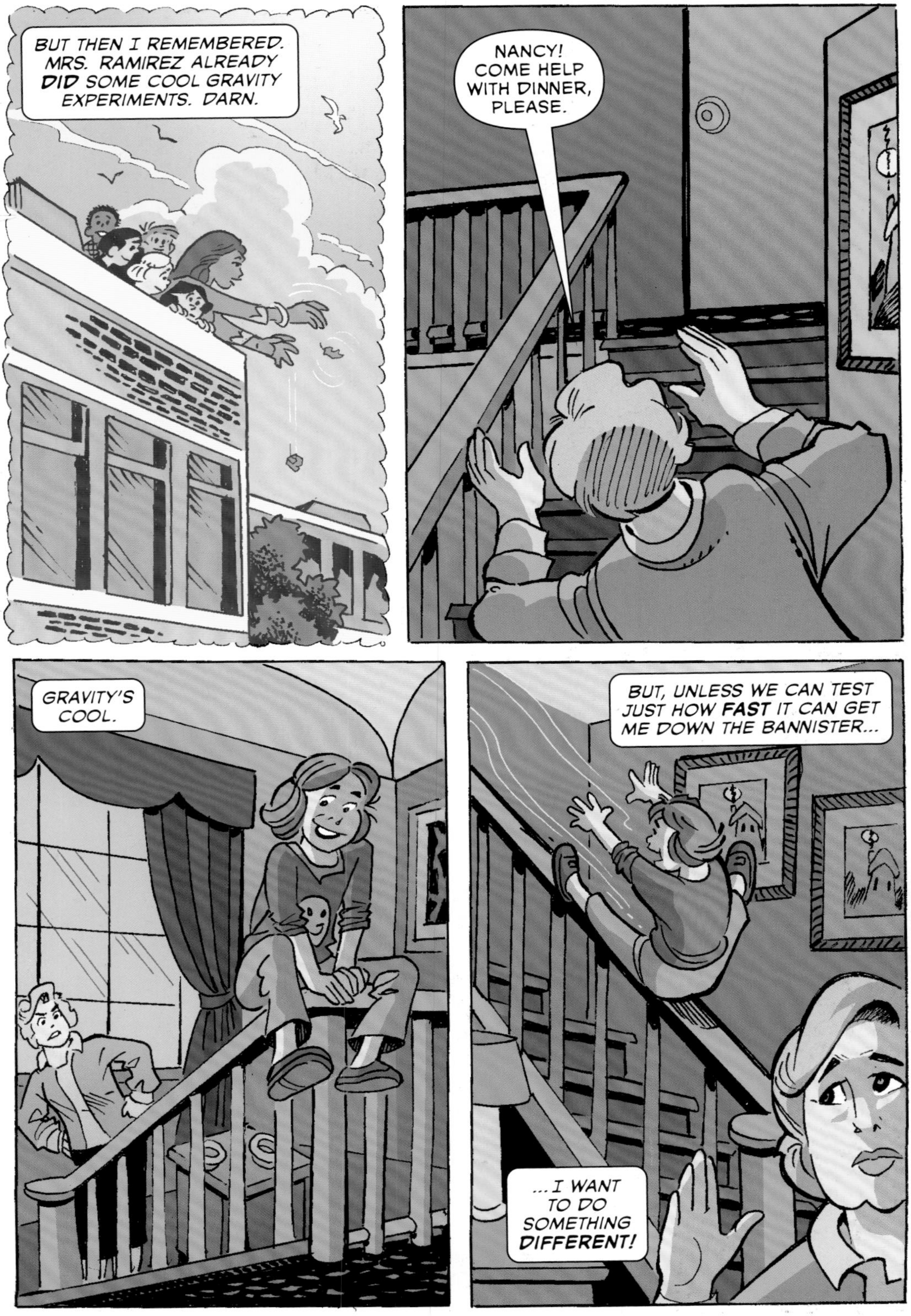
BUT THEN I REMEMBERED. MRS. RAMIREZ ALREADY DID SOME COOL GRAVITY EXPERIMENTS. DARN.
NANCY! COME HELP WITH DINNER, PLEASE.
GRAVITY'S COOL.
BUT, UNLESS WE CAN TEST JUST HOW FAST IT CAN GET ME DOWN THE BANNISTER...
...I WANT TO DO SOMETHING DIFFERENT!

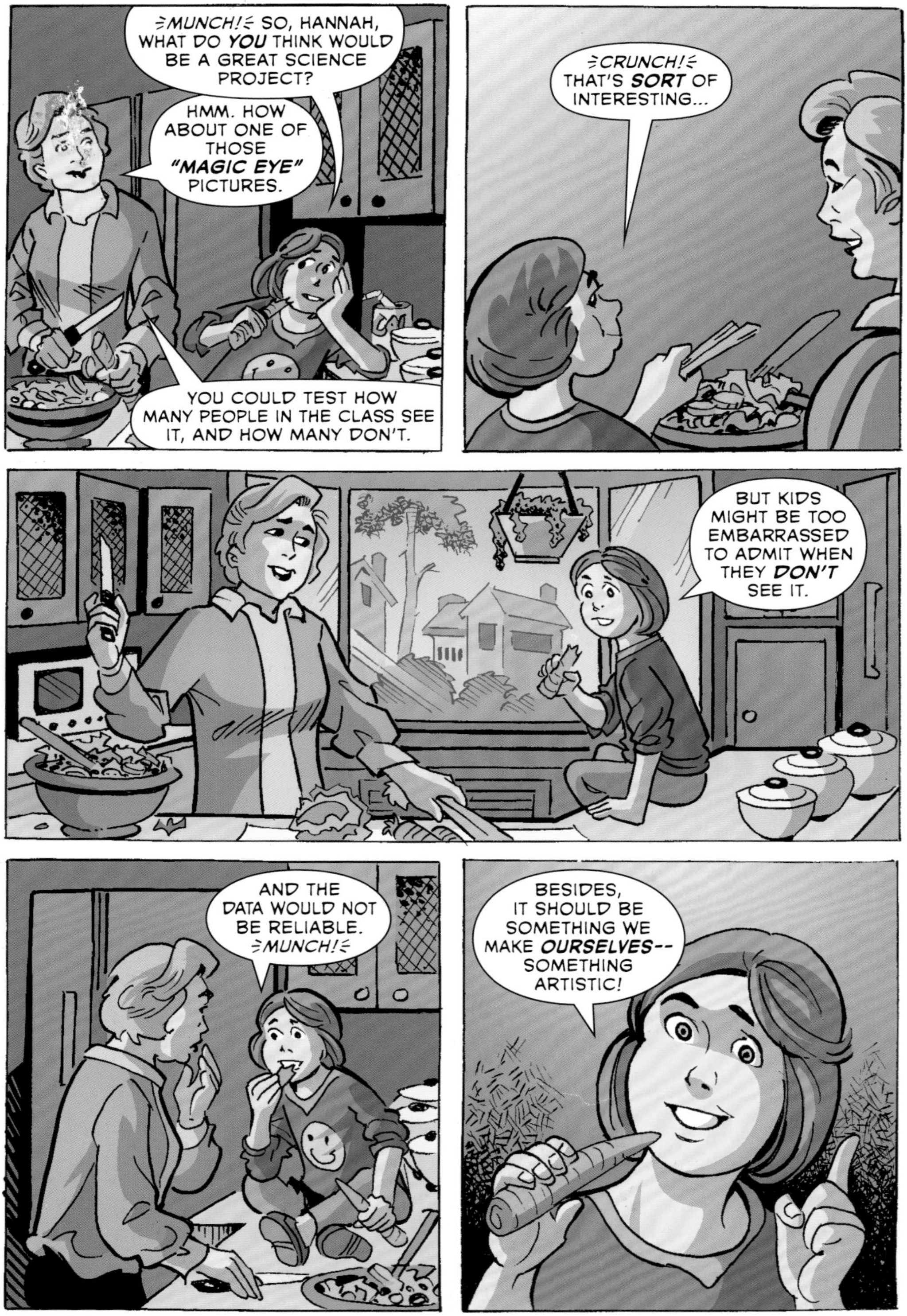

⩶MUNCH!⩶ SO, HANNAH, WHAT DO *YOU* THINK WOULD BE A GREAT SCIENCE PROJECT?
HMM. HOW ABOUT ONE OF THOSE *"MAGIC EYE"* PICTURES.
YOU COULD TEST HOW MANY PEOPLE IN THE CLASS SEE IT, AND HOW MANY DON'T.
⩶CRUNCH!⩶ THAT'S *SORT* OF INTERESTING...
BUT KIDS MIGHT BE TOO EMBARRASSED TO ADMIT WHEN THEY *DON'T* SEE IT.
AND THE DATA WOULD NOT BE RELIABLE. ⩶MUNCH!⩶
BESIDES, IT SHOULD BE SOMETHING WE MAKE *OURSELVES*-- SOMETHING ARTISTIC!

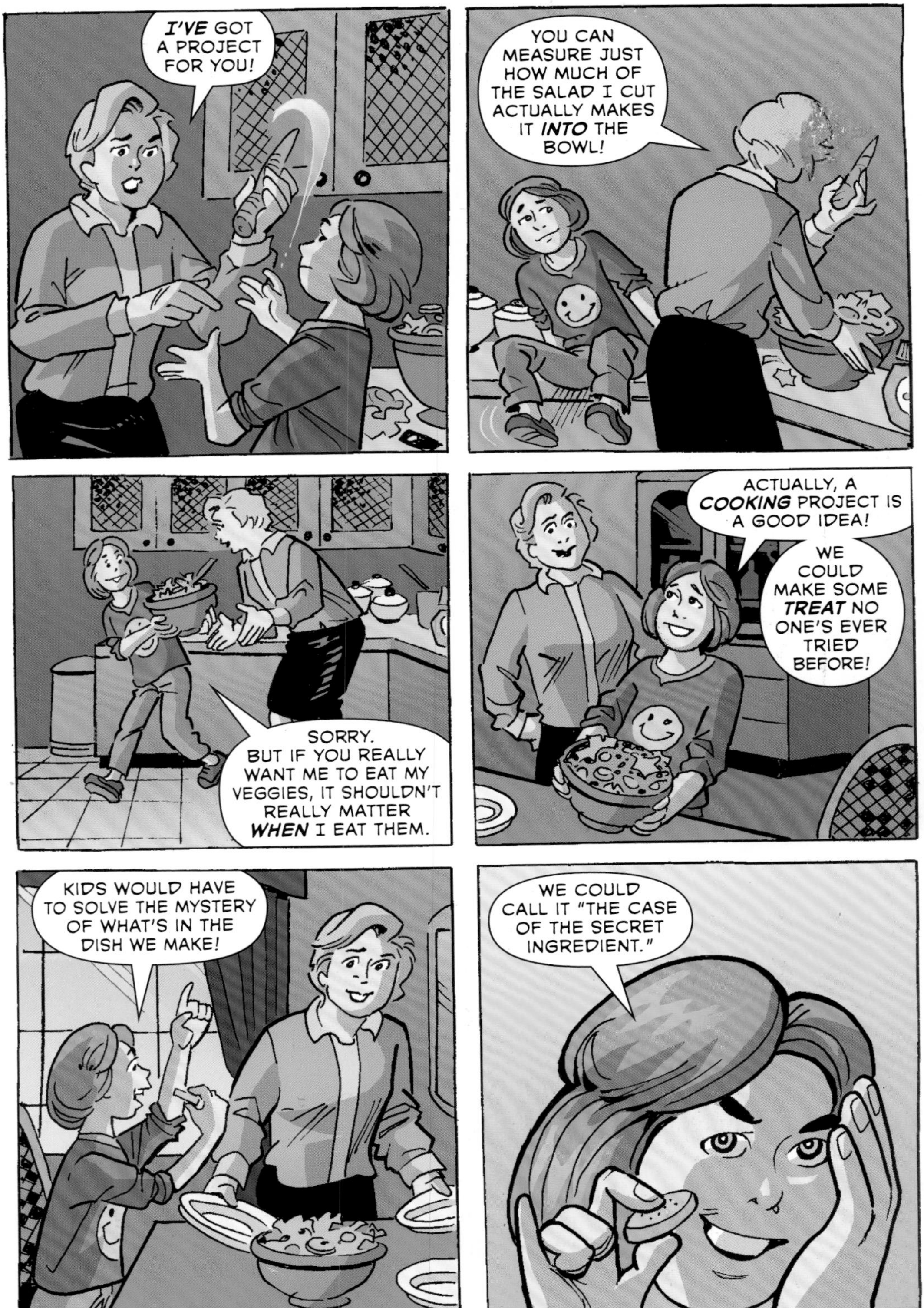
I'VE GOT A PROJECT FOR YOU!
YOU CAN MEASURE JUST HOW MUCH OF THE SALAD I CUT ACTUALLY MAKES IT INTO THE BOWL!
SORRY. BUT IF YOU REALLY WANT ME TO EAT MY VEGGIES, IT SHOULDN'T REALLY MATTER WHEN I EAT THEM.
ACTUALLY, A COOKING PROJECT IS A GOOD IDEA!
WE COULD MAKE SOME TREAT NO ONE'S EVER TRIED BEFORE!
KIDS WOULD HAVE TO SOLVE THE MYSTERY OF WHAT'S IN THE DISH WE MAKE!
WE COULD CALL IT "THE CASE OF THE SECRET INGREDIENT."

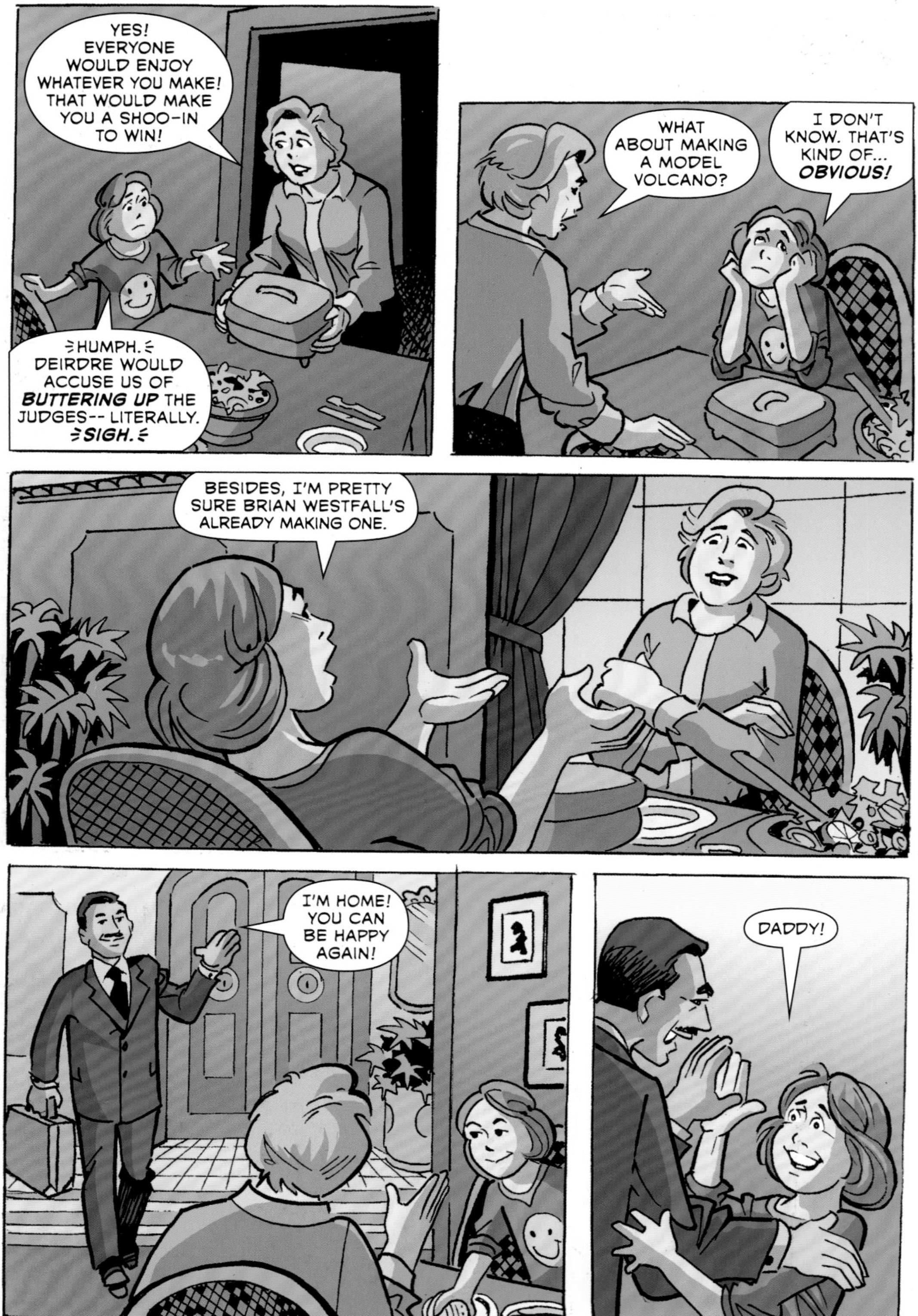
YES! EVERYONE WOULD ENJOY WHATEVER YOU MAKE! THAT WOULD MAKE YOU A SHOO-IN TO WIN!
HUMPH. DEIRDRE WOULD ACCUSE US OF BUTTERING UP THE JUDGES-- LITERALLY. SIGH.
WHAT ABOUT MAKING A MODEL VOLCANO?
I DON'T KNOW. THAT'S KIND OF... OBVIOUS!
BESIDES, I'M PRETTY SURE BRIAN WESTFALL'S ALREADY MAKING ONE.
I'M HOME! YOU CAN BE HAPPY AGAIN!
DADDY!

THAT'S MY DAD, **CARSON DREW.** HE'S A LAWYER. HANNAH AND I ARE ALWAYS SO HAPPY WHEN HE COMES HOME FROM A BUSINESS TRIP!

HE TELLS THE **BEST** STORIES ABOUT HIS REALLY RICH AND KINDA WACKY CLIENTS.

SO, I TOLD RAJNEESH IF HE'D JUST BUILT A **FLOOD DRAIN,** HIS SALT-WATER WAVE POOL WOULDN'T HAVE FLOODED HIS NEIGHBOR'S SUGAR REFINERY!

HAH! THAT'S A LOT OF WET SUGAR! THEY SHOULD HAVE GOTTEN TOGETHER AND MADE TAFFY!

RIGHT, NANCY?

HUH?

USUALLY, I HANG ON DAD'S EVERY WORD.

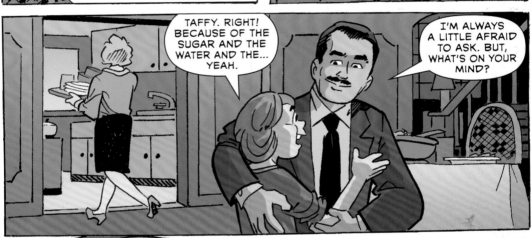

TAFFY. RIGHT! BECAUSE OF THE SUGAR AND THE WATER AND THE... YEAH.

I'M ALWAYS A LITTLE AFRAID TO ASK. BUT, WHAT'S ON YOUR MIND?

I SUDDENLY REALIZED, I COULD ASK **HIM** FOR HELP!

DAD, WHAT KIND OF SCIENCE PROJECTS DID **YOU** DO WHEN YOU WERE MY AGE?

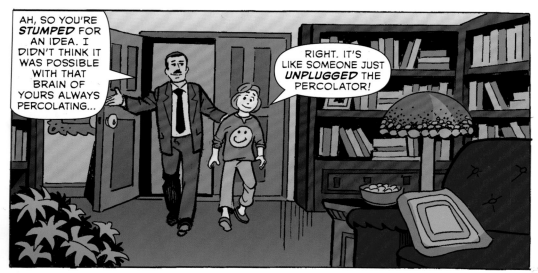

AH, SO YOU'RE *STUMPED* FOR AN IDEA. I DIDN'T THINK IT WAS POSSIBLE WITH THAT BRAIN OF YOURS ALWAYS PERCOLATING...

RIGHT. IT'S LIKE SOMEONE JUST *UNPLUGGED* THE PERCOLATOR!

I THINK I CAN HELP.

REALLY?

CERTAINLY. NOW, LET'S SEE. MY FATHER *PHOTOGRAPHED* ALL MY ACADEMIC ACHIEVEMENTS.

THIS WAS GREAT! SOME-TIMES I HELP MY DAD OUT WITH *HIS* WORK, SO I THINK HE FELT GOOD ABOUT HELPING ME WITH *MINE!* AND SO DID I.

THERE IT IS. THE *BEST* DARN SCIENCE PROJECT THE FOURTH GRADE HAD EVER SEEN.

OH, GORDON CRAWFORD'S *BICYCLE GENERATOR* WAS ALL RIGHT, AND ZEFFA WOOLWINE'S *MOUSE MAZE* WAS FINE...

BUT ALL THE KIDS OOH'ED AND AHHH'D WHEN THEY SAW MY WORKING MODEL OF...

WHAT? WHAT DID YOU MAKE?

A VOLCANO?

⋛SIGH.⋚

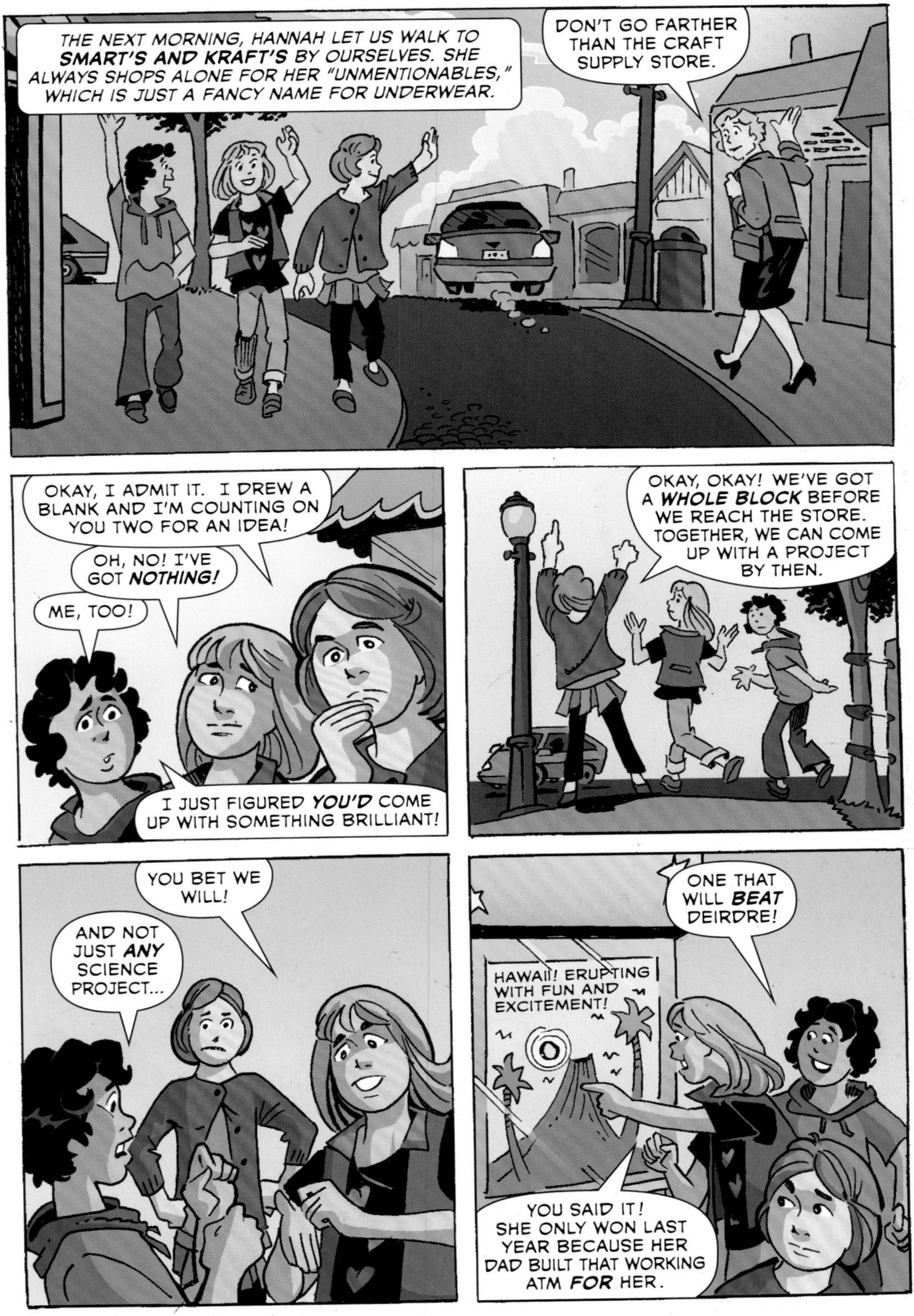
THE NEXT MORNING, HANNAH LET US WALK TO SMART'S AND KRAFT'S BY OURSELVES. SHE ALWAYS SHOPS ALONE FOR HER "UNMENTIONABLES," WHICH IS JUST A FANCY NAME FOR UNDERWEAR.
DON'T GO FARTHER THAN THE CRAFT SUPPLY STORE.
OKAY, I ADMIT IT. I DREW A BLANK AND I'M COUNTING ON YOU TWO FOR AN IDEA!
OH, NO! I'VE GOT NOTHING!
ME, TOO!
I JUST FIGURED YOU'D COME UP WITH SOMETHING BRILLIANT!
OKAY, OKAY! WE'VE GOT A WHOLE BLOCK BEFORE WE REACH THE STORE. TOGETHER, WE CAN COME UP WITH A PROJECT BY THEN.
YOU BET WE WILL!
AND NOT JUST ANY SCIENCE PROJECT...
ONE THAT WILL BEAT DEIRDRE!
HAWAII! ERUPTING WITH FUN AND EXCITEMENT!
YOU SAID IT! SHE ONLY WON LAST YEAR BECAUSE HER DAD BUILT THAT WORKING ATM FOR HER.

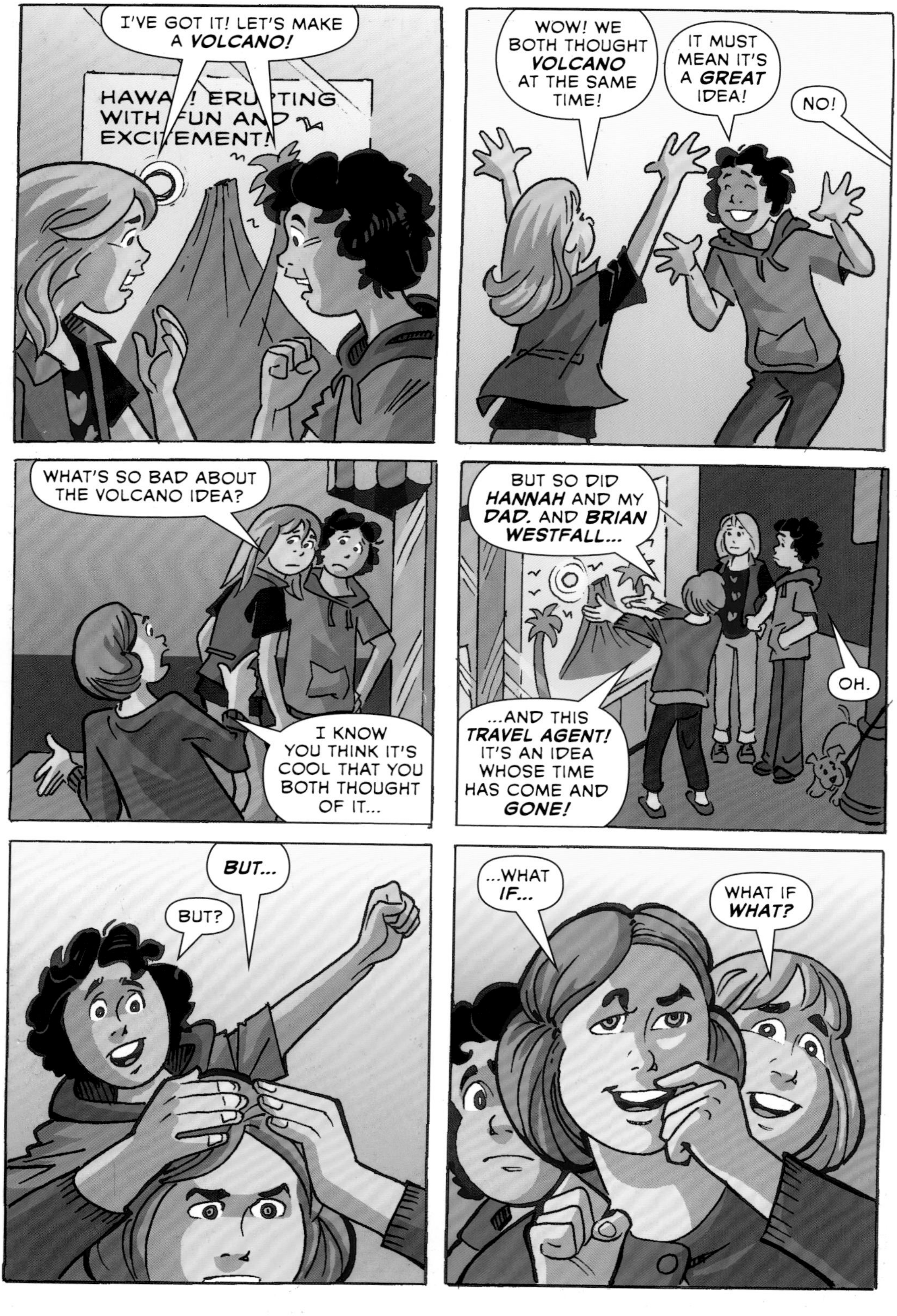
I'VE GOT IT! LET'S MAKE A VOLCANO!
HAWA ! ERU TING WITH FUN AN EXCI EMENT!
WOW! WE BOTH THOUGHT VOLCANO AT THE SAME TIME!
IT MUST MEAN IT'S A GREAT IDEA!
NO!
WHAT'S SO BAD ABOUT THE VOLCANO IDEA?
I KNOW YOU THINK IT'S COOL THAT YOU BOTH THOUGHT OF IT...
BUT SO DID HANNAH AND MY DAD. AND BRIAN WESTFALL...
...AND THIS TRAVEL AGENT! IT'S AN IDEA WHOSE TIME HAS COME AND GONE!
OH.
BUT?
BUT...
...WHAT IF...
WHAT IF WHAT?

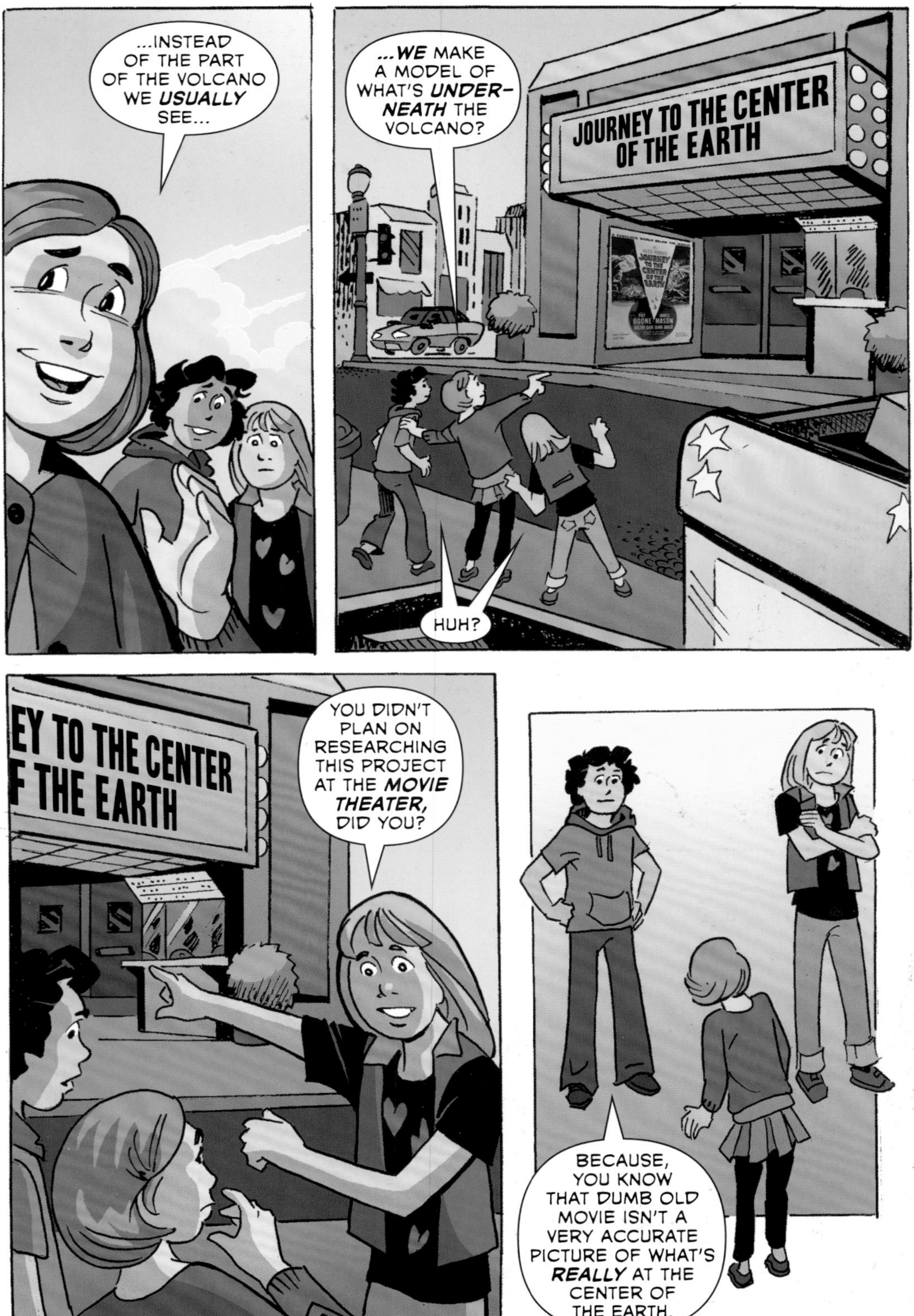
...INSTEAD OF THE PART OF THE VOLCANO WE *USUALLY* SEE...
...WE MAKE A MODEL OF WHAT'S ***UNDER-NEATH*** THE VOLCANO?
JOURNEY TO THE CENTER OF THE EARTH
HUH?
EY TO THE CENTER
F THE EARTH
YOU DIDN'T PLAN ON RESEARCHING THIS PROJECT AT THE ***MOVIE THEATER,*** DID YOU?
BECAUSE, YOU KNOW THAT DUMB OLD MOVIE ISN'T A VERY ACCURATE PICTURE OF WHAT'S ***REALLY*** AT THE CENTER OF THE EARTH.

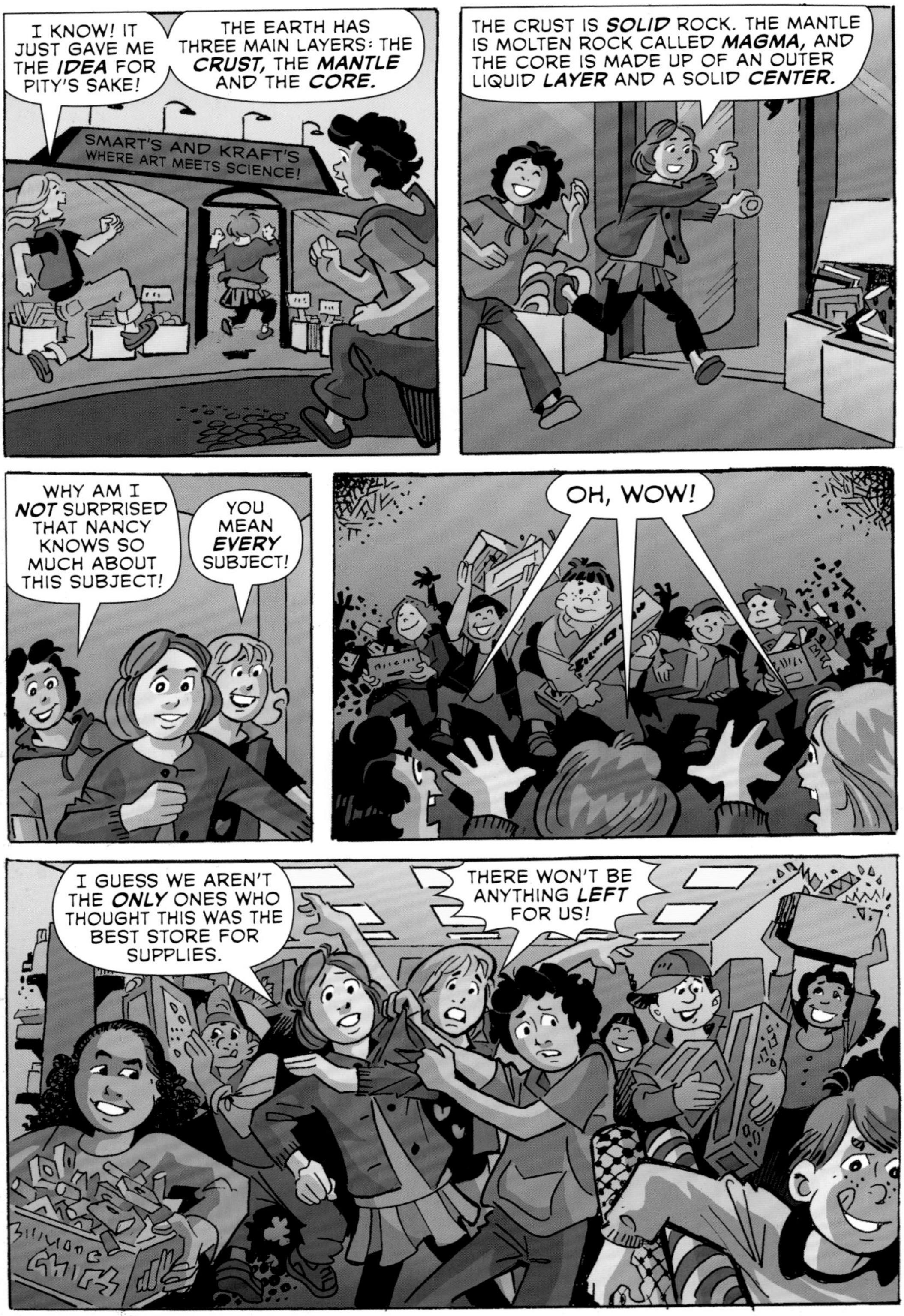
I KNOW! IT JUST GAVE ME THE *IDEA* FOR PITY'S SAKE!
THE EARTH HAS THREE MAIN LAYERS: THE *CRUST,* THE *MANTLE* AND THE *CORE.*
SMART'S AND KRAFT'S
WHERE ART MEETS SCIENCE!
THE CRUST IS *SOLID* ROCK. THE MANTLE IS MOLTEN ROCK CALLED *MAGMA,* AND THE CORE IS MADE UP OF AN OUTER LIQUID *LAYER* AND A SOLID *CENTER.*
WHY AM I *NOT* SURPRISED THAT NANCY KNOWS SO MUCH ABOUT THIS SUBJECT!
YOU MEAN *EVERY* SUBJECT!
OH, WOW!
I GUESS WE AREN'T THE *ONLY* ONES WHO THOUGHT THIS WAS THE BEST STORE FOR SUPPLIES.
THERE WON'T BE ANYTHING *LEFT* FOR US!

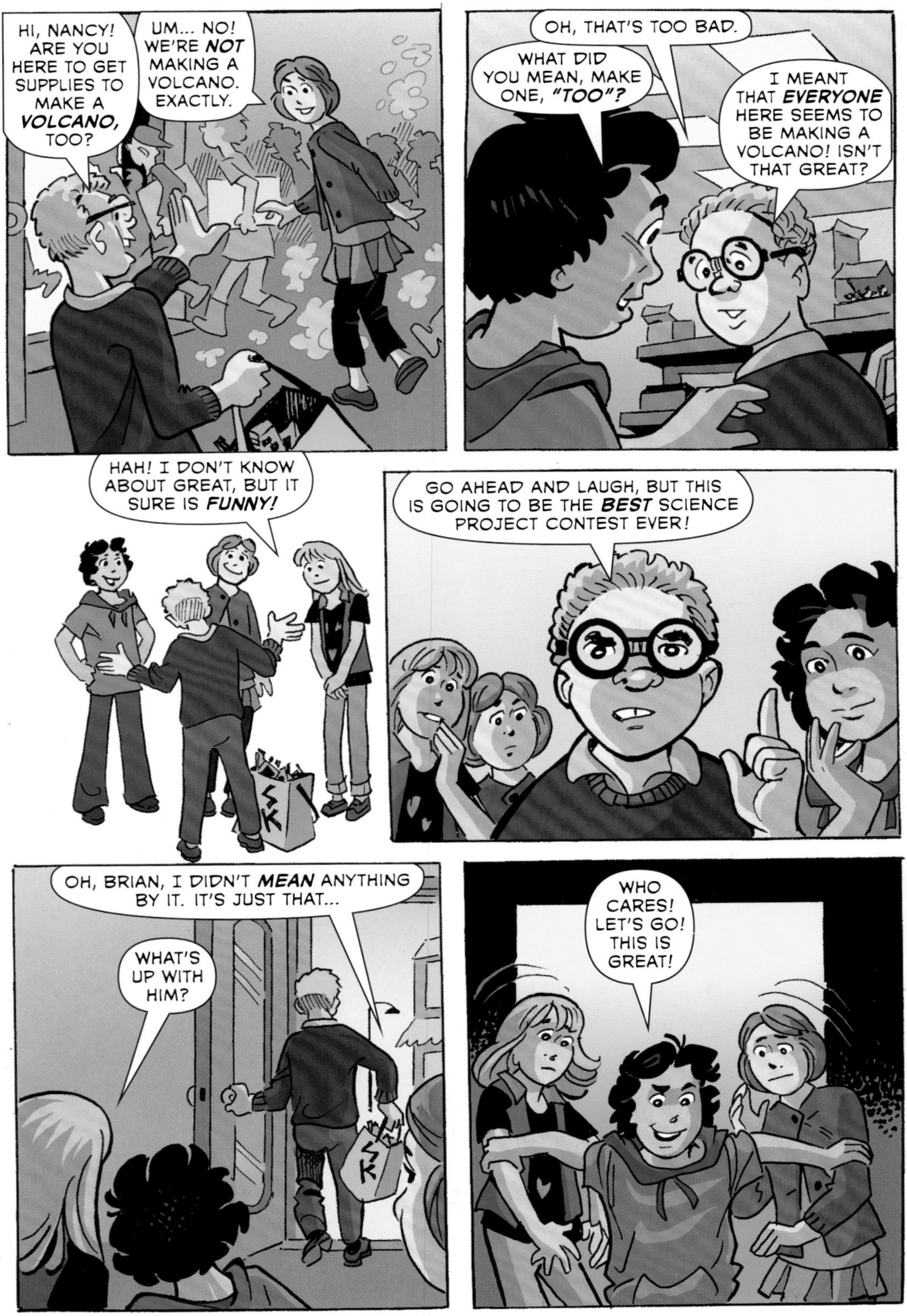
HI, NANCY! ARE YOU HERE TO GET SUPPLIES TO MAKE A **VOLCANO,** TOO?
UM... NO! WE'RE **NOT** MAKING A VOLCANO. EXACTLY.
OH, THAT'S TOO BAD.
WHAT DID YOU MEAN, MAKE ONE, **"TOO"?**
I MEANT THAT **EVERYONE** HERE SEEMS TO BE MAKING A VOLCANO! ISN'T THAT GREAT?
HAH! I DON'T KNOW ABOUT GREAT, BUT IT SURE IS **FUNNY!**
GO AHEAD AND LAUGH, BUT THIS IS GOING TO BE THE **BEST** SCIENCE PROJECT CONTEST EVER!
OH, BRIAN, I DIDN'T **MEAN** ANYTHING BY IT. IT'S JUST THAT...
WHAT'S UP WITH HIM?
WHO CARES! LET'S GO! THIS IS GREAT!

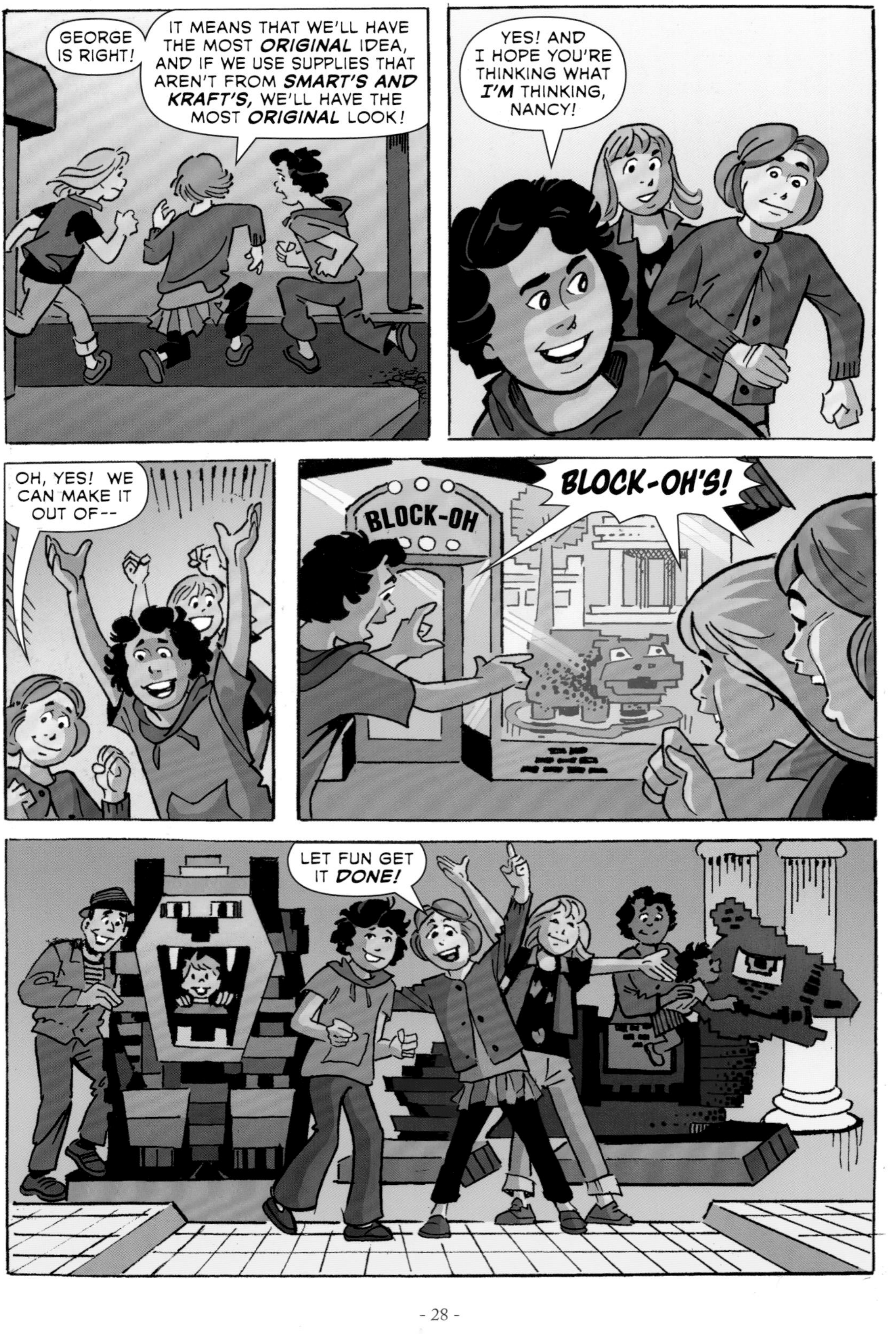
GEORGE IS RIGHT!
IT MEANS THAT WE'LL HAVE THE MOST ORIGINAL IDEA, AND IF WE USE SUPPLIES THAT AREN'T FROM SMART'S AND KRAFT'S, WE'LL HAVE THE MOST ORIGINAL LOOK!
YES! AND I HOPE YOU'RE THINKING WHAT I'M THINKING, NANCY!
OH, YES! WE CAN MAKE IT OUT OF--
BLOCK-OH
BLOCK-OH'S!
LET FUN GET IT DONE!

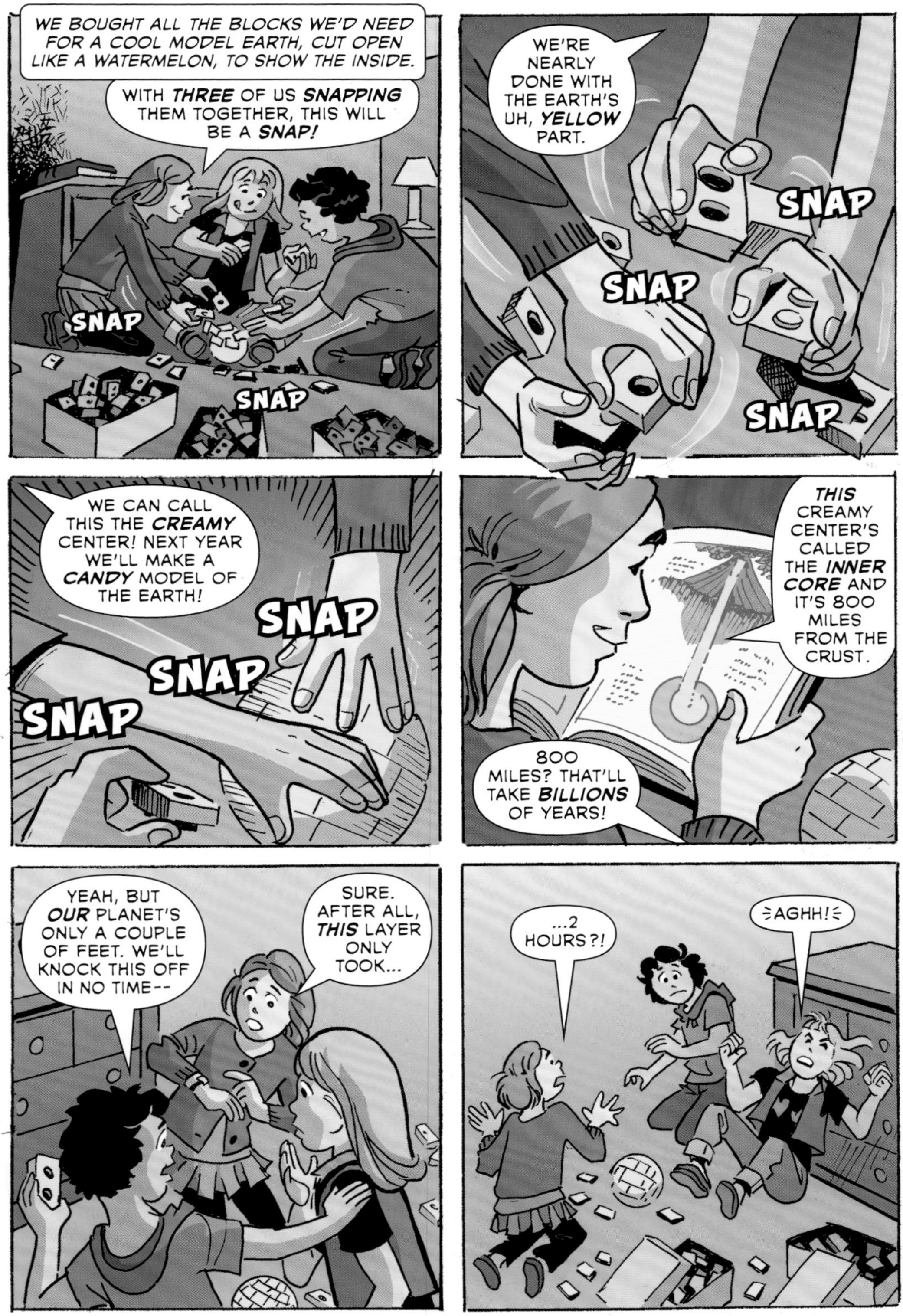
WE BOUGHT ALL THE BLOCKS WE'D NEED FOR A COOL MODEL EARTH, CUT OPEN LIKE A WATERMELON, TO SHOW THE INSIDE.
WITH THREE OF US SNAPPING THEM TOGETHER, THIS WILL BE A SNAP!
SNAP
SNAP
WE'RE NEARLY DONE WITH THE EARTH'S UH, YELLOW PART.
SNAP
SNAP
SNAP
WE CAN CALL THIS THE CREAMY CENTER! NEXT YEAR WE'LL MAKE A CANDY MODEL OF THE EARTH!
SNAP
SNAP
SNAP
THIS CREAMY CENTER'S CALLED THE INNER CORE AND IT'S 800 MILES FROM THE CRUST.
800 MILES? THAT'LL TAKE BILLIONS OF YEARS!
YEAH, BUT OUR PLANET'S ONLY A COUPLE OF FEET. WE'LL KNOCK THIS OFF IN NO TIME--
SURE. AFTER ALL, THIS LAYER ONLY TOOK...
...2 HOURS?!
AGHH!

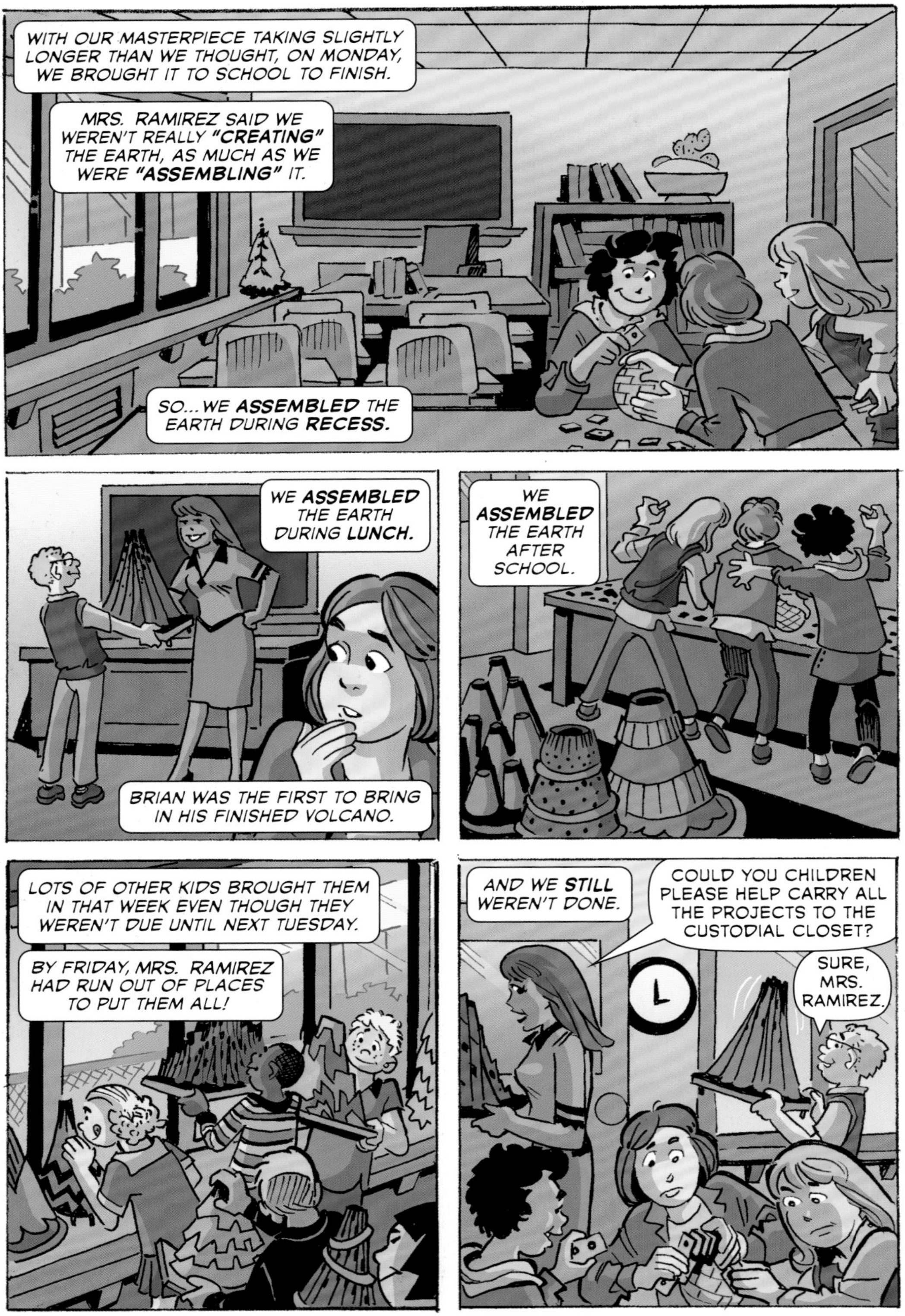
WITH OUR MASTERPIECE TAKING SLIGHTLY LONGER THAN WE THOUGHT, ON MONDAY, WE BROUGHT IT TO SCHOOL TO FINISH.
MRS. RAMIREZ SAID WE WEREN'T REALLY "CREATING" THE EARTH, AS MUCH AS WE WERE "ASSEMBLING" IT.
SO...WE ASSEMBLED THE EARTH DURING RECESS.
WE ASSEMBLED THE EARTH DURING LUNCH.
BRIAN WAS THE FIRST TO BRING IN HIS FINISHED VOLCANO.
WE ASSEMBLED THE EARTH AFTER SCHOOL.
LOTS OF OTHER KIDS BROUGHT THEM IN THAT WEEK EVEN THOUGH THEY WEREN'T DUE UNTIL NEXT TUESDAY.
BY FRIDAY, MRS. RAMIREZ HAD RUN OUT OF PLACES TO PUT THEM ALL!
AND WE STILL WEREN'T DONE.
COULD YOU CHILDREN PLEASE HELP CARRY ALL THE PROJECTS TO THE CUSTODIAL CLOSET?
SURE, MRS. RAMIREZ.

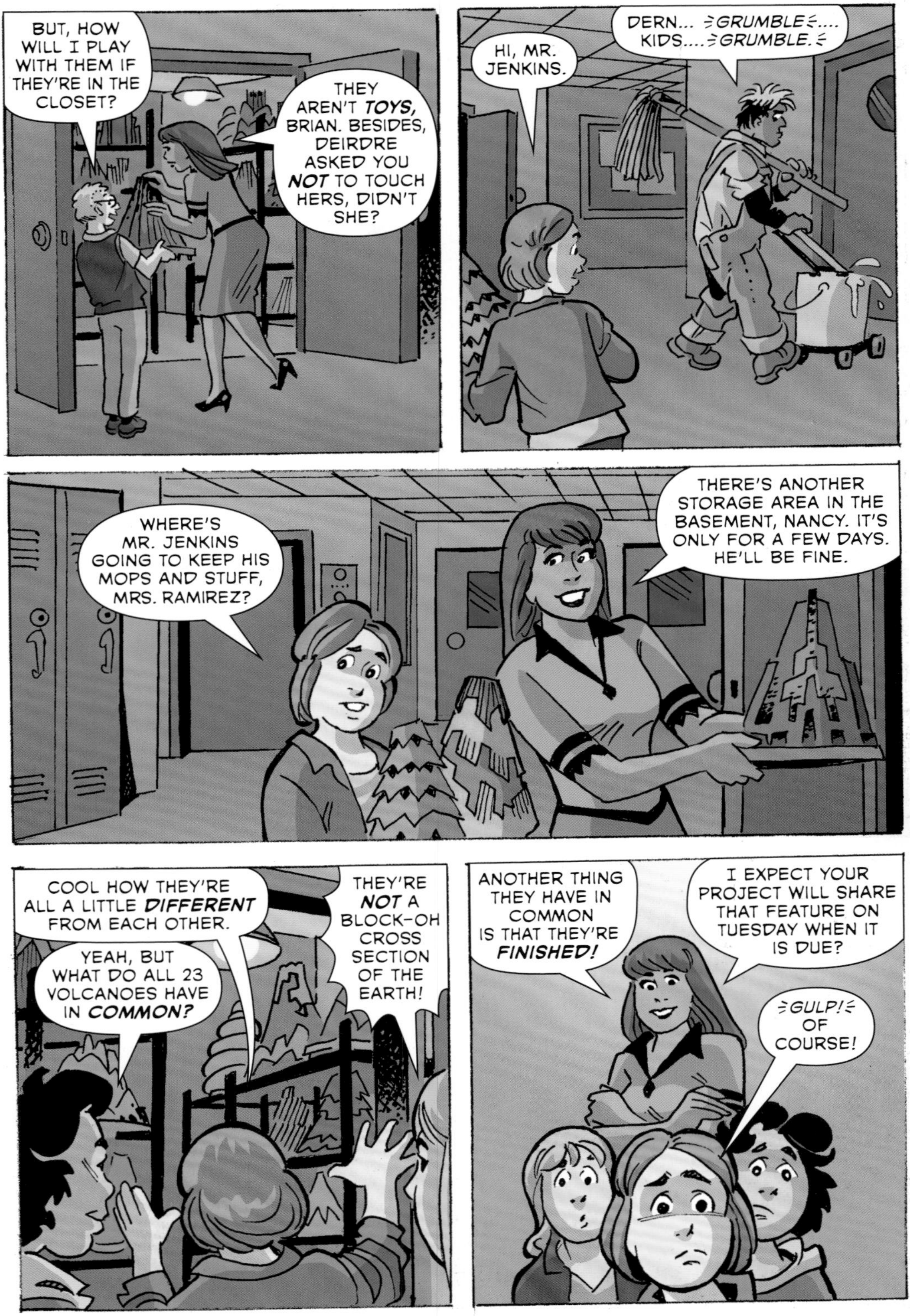
BUT, HOW WILL I PLAY WITH THEM IF THEY'RE IN THE CLOSET?
THEY AREN'T TOYS, BRIAN. BESIDES, DEIRDRE ASKED YOU NOT TO TOUCH HERS, DIDN'T SHE?
HI, MR. JENKINS.
DERN... ≷GRUMBLE≶.... KIDS....≷GRUMBLE.≶
WHERE'S MR. JENKINS GOING TO KEEP HIS MOPS AND STUFF, MRS. RAMIREZ?
THERE'S ANOTHER STORAGE AREA IN THE BASEMENT, NANCY. IT'S ONLY FOR A FEW DAYS. HE'LL BE FINE.
COOL HOW THEY'RE ALL A LITTLE DIFFERENT FROM EACH OTHER.
YEAH, BUT WHAT DO ALL 23 VOLCANOES HAVE IN COMMON?
THEY'RE NOT A BLOCK-OH CROSS SECTION OF THE EARTH!
ANOTHER THING THEY HAVE IN COMMON IS THAT THEY'RE FINISHED!
I EXPECT YOUR PROJECT WILL SHARE THAT FEATURE ON TUESDAY WHEN IT IS DUE?
≷GULP!≶ OF COURSE!

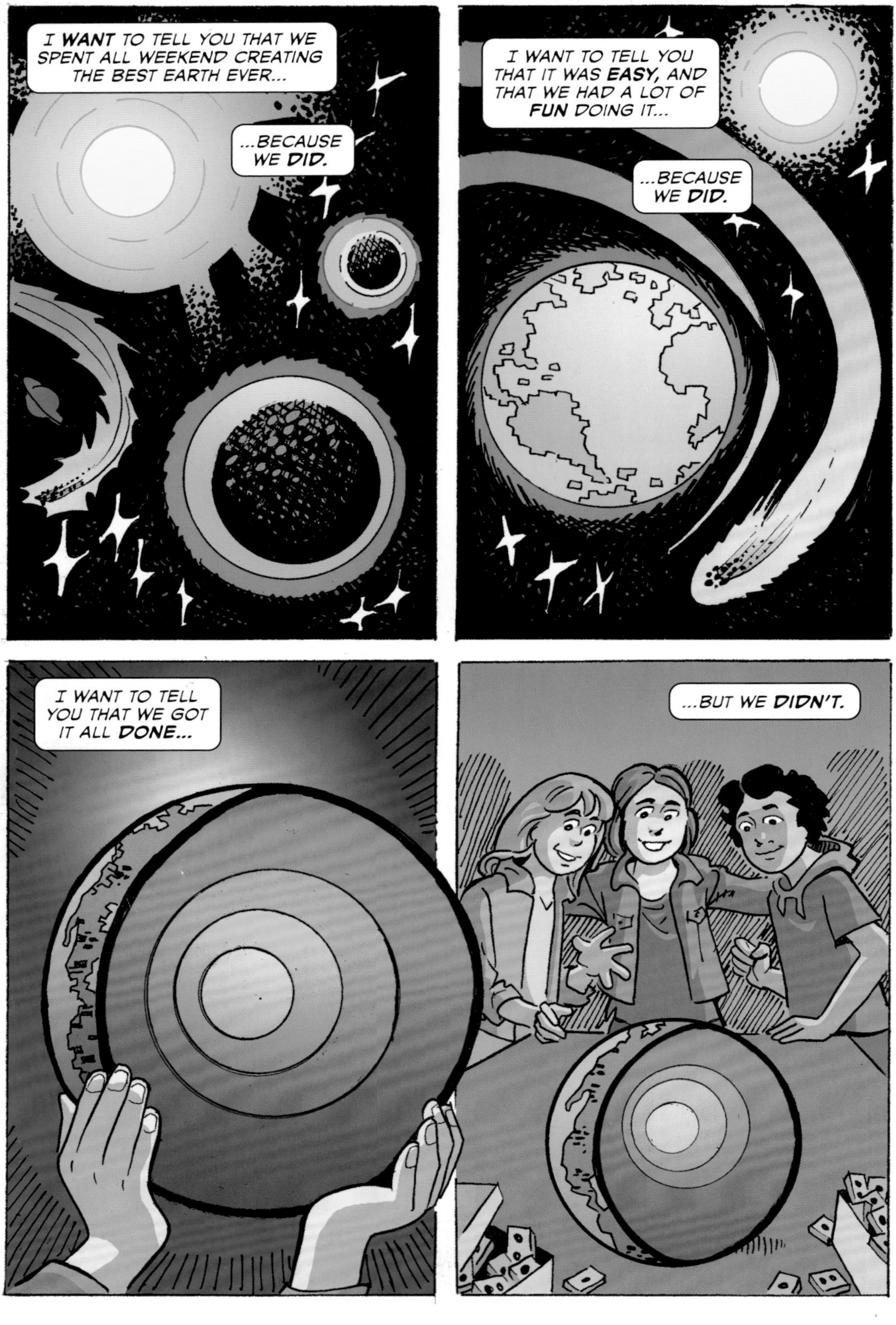
I WANT TO TELL YOU THAT WE SPENT ALL WEEKEND CREATING THE BEST EARTH EVER...
...BECAUSE WE DID.
I WANT TO TELL YOU THAT IT WAS EASY, AND THAT WE HAD A LOT OF FUN DOING IT...
...BECAUSE WE DID.
I WANT TO TELL YOU THAT WE GOT IT ALL DONE...
...BUT WE DIDN'T.

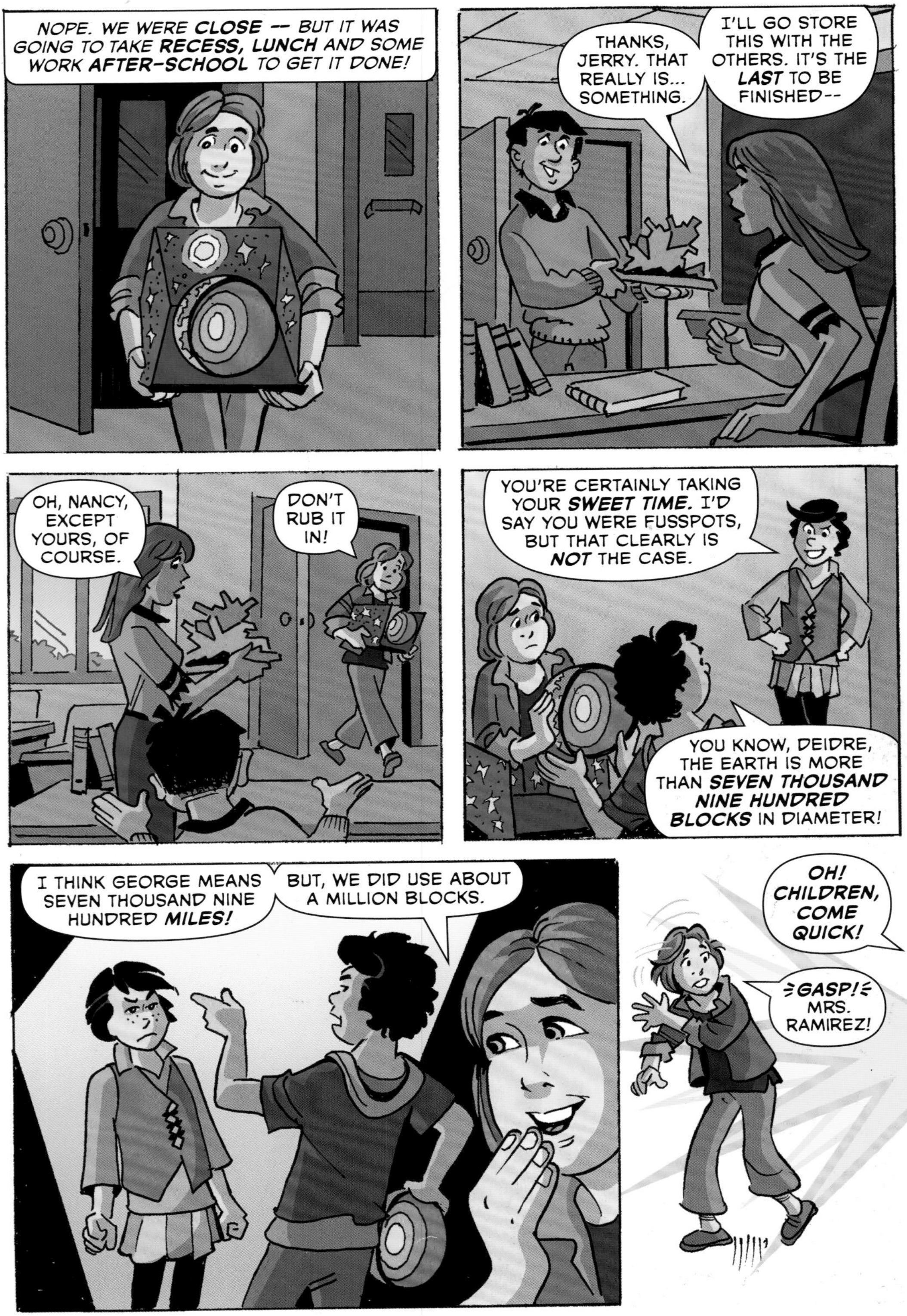
NOPE. WE WERE CLOSE -- BUT IT WAS GOING TO TAKE RECESS, LUNCH AND SOME WORK AFTER-SCHOOL TO GET IT DONE!
THANKS, JERRY. THAT REALLY IS... SOMETHING.
I'LL GO STORE THIS WITH THE OTHERS. IT'S THE LAST TO BE FINISHED--
OH, NANCY, EXCEPT YOURS, OF COURSE.
DON'T RUB IT IN!
YOU'RE CERTAINLY TAKING YOUR SWEET TIME. I'D SAY YOU WERE FUSSPOTS, BUT THAT CLEARLY IS NOT THE CASE.
YOU KNOW, DEIDRE, THE EARTH IS MORE THAN SEVEN THOUSAND NINE HUNDRED BLOCKS IN DIAMETER!
I THINK GEORGE MEANS SEVEN THOUSAND NINE HUNDRED MILES!
BUT, WE DID USE ABOUT A MILLION BLOCKS.
OH! CHILDREN, COME QUICK!
GASP! MRS. RAMIREZ!

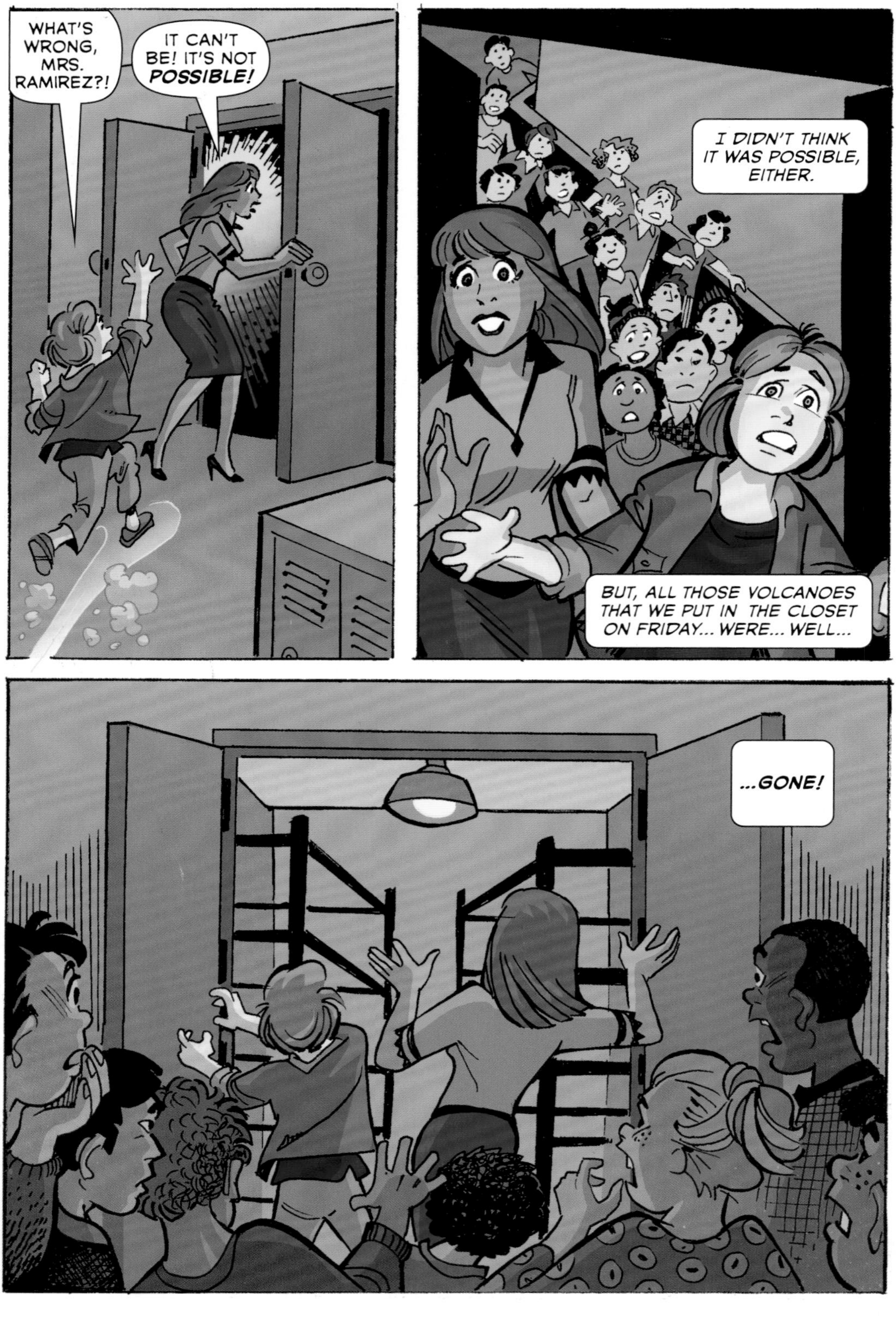
WHAT'S WRONG, MRS. RAMIREZ?!
IT CAN'T BE! IT'S NOT POSSIBLE!
I DIDN'T THINK IT WAS POSSIBLE, EITHER.
BUT, ALL THOSE VOLCANOES THAT WE PUT IN THE CLOSET ON FRIDAY... WERE... WELL...
...GONE!

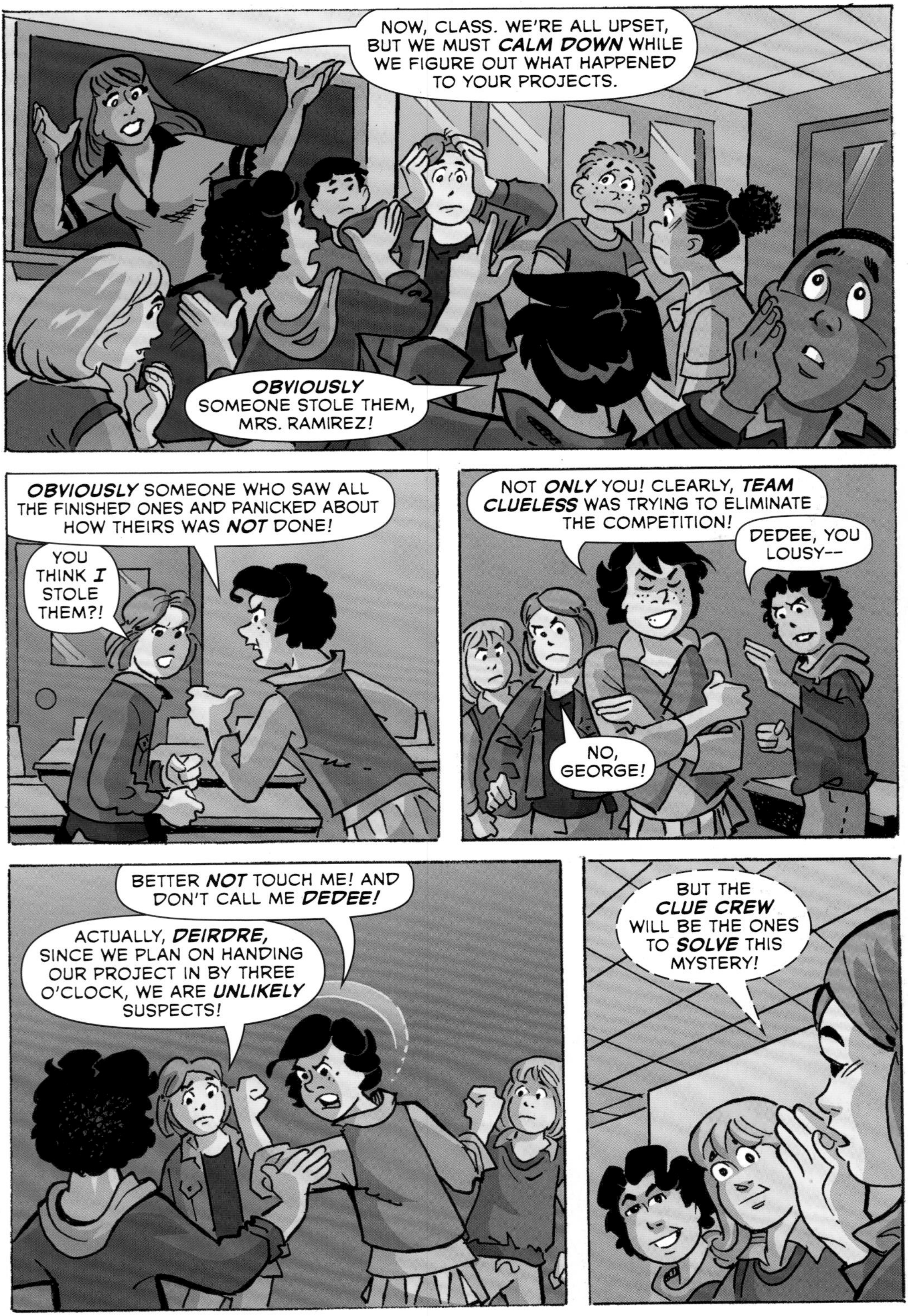
NOW, CLASS. WE'RE ALL UPSET, BUT WE MUST CALM DOWN WHILE WE FIGURE OUT WHAT HAPPENED TO YOUR PROJECTS.
OBVIOUSLY SOMEONE STOLE THEM, MRS. RAMIREZ!
OBVIOUSLY SOMEONE WHO SAW ALL THE FINISHED ONES AND PANICKED ABOUT HOW THEIRS WAS NOT DONE!
YOU THINK I STOLE THEM?!
NOT ONLY YOU! CLEARLY, TEAM CLUELESS WAS TRYING TO ELIMINATE THE COMPETITION!
DEDEE, YOU LOUSY--
NO, GEORGE!
BETTER NOT TOUCH ME! AND DON'T CALL ME DEDEE!
ACTUALLY, DEIRDRE, SINCE WE PLAN ON HANDING OUR PROJECT IN BY THREE O'CLOCK, WE ARE UNLIKELY SUSPECTS!
BUT THE CLUE CREW WILL BE THE ONES TO SOLVE THIS MYSTERY!

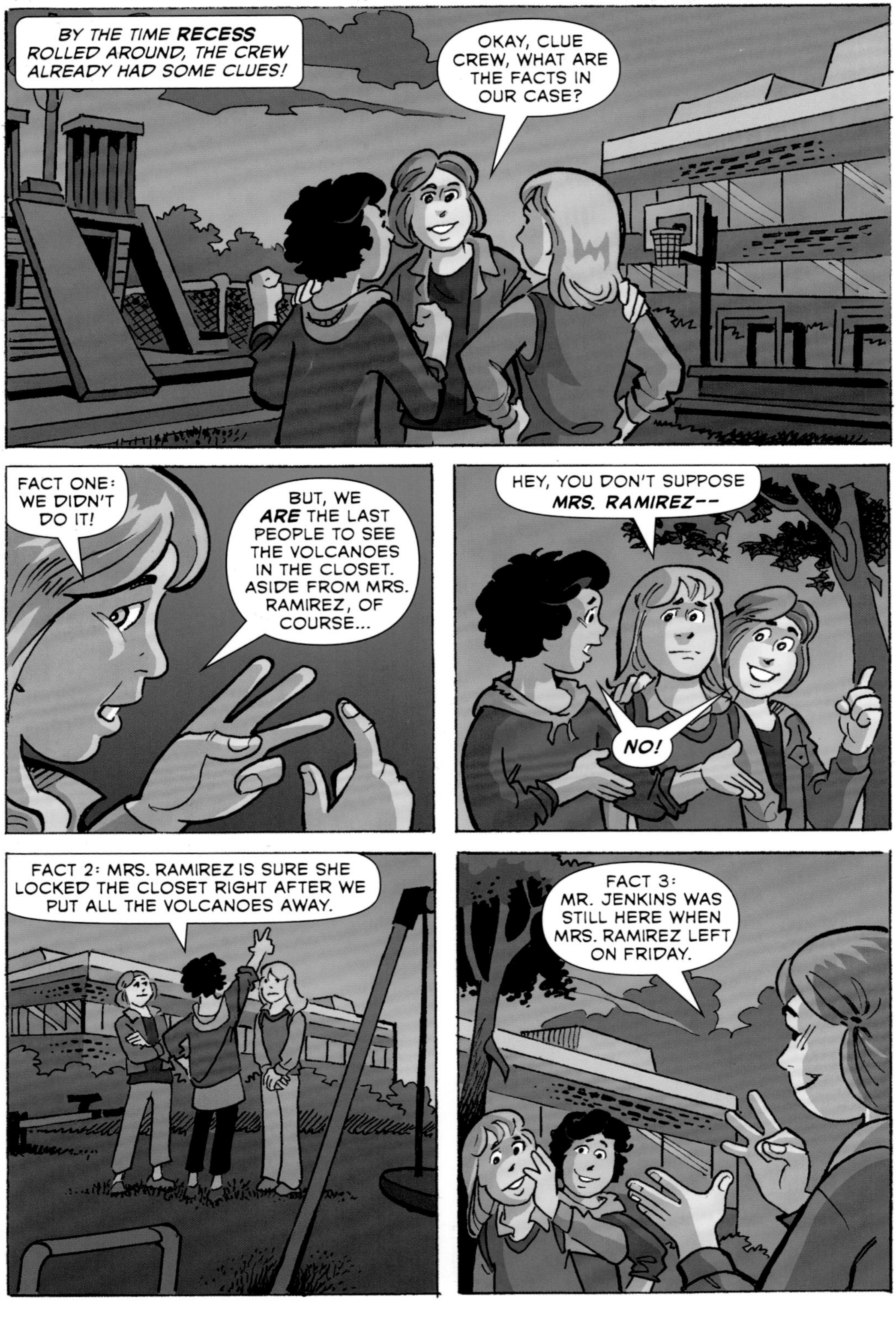
BY THE TIME RECESS ROLLED AROUND, THE CREW ALREADY HAD SOME CLUES!
OKAY, CLUE CREW, WHAT ARE THE FACTS IN OUR CASE?
FACT ONE: WE DIDN'T DO IT!
BUT, WE ARE THE LAST PEOPLE TO SEE THE VOLCANOES IN THE CLOSET. ASIDE FROM MRS. RAMIREZ, OF COURSE...
HEY, YOU DON'T SUPPOSE MRS. RAMIREZ--
NO!
FACT 2: MRS. RAMIREZ IS SURE SHE LOCKED THE CLOSET RIGHT AFTER WE PUT ALL THE VOLCANOES AWAY.
FACT 3: MR. JENKINS WAS STILL HERE WHEN MRS. RAMIREZ LEFT ON FRIDAY.

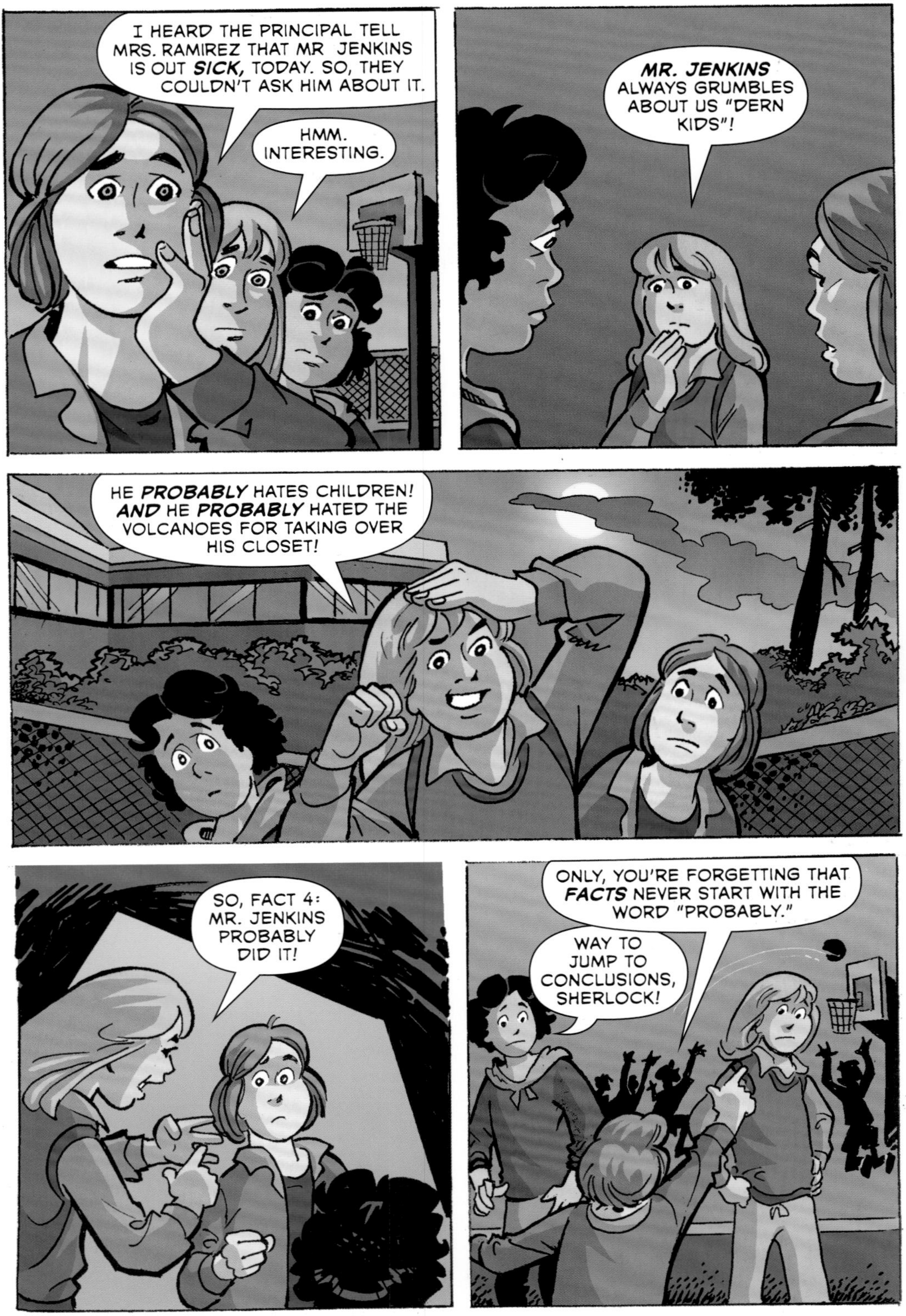
I HEARD THE PRINCIPAL TELL MRS. RAMIREZ THAT MR JENKINS IS OUT SICK, TODAY. SO, THEY COULDN'T ASK HIM ABOUT IT.
HMM. INTERESTING.
MR. JENKINS ALWAYS GRUMBLES ABOUT US "DERN KIDS"!
HE PROBABLY HATES CHILDREN! AND HE PROBABLY HATED THE VOLCANOES FOR TAKING OVER HIS CLOSET!
SO, FACT 4: MR. JENKINS PROBABLY DID IT!
ONLY, YOU'RE FORGETTING THAT FACTS NEVER START WITH THE WORD "PROBABLY."
WAY TO JUMP TO CONCLUSIONS, SHERLOCK!

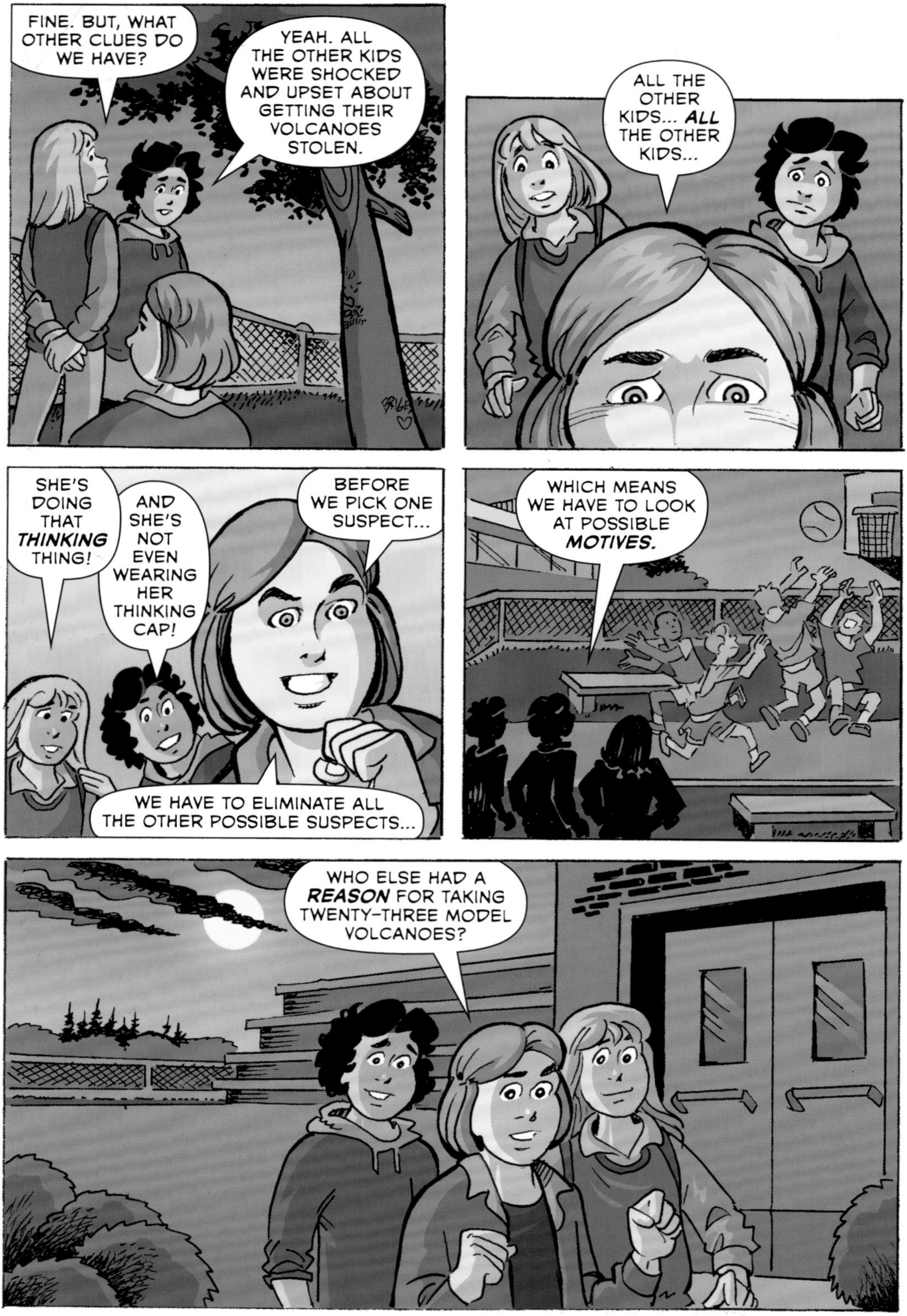
FINE. BUT, WHAT OTHER CLUES DO WE HAVE?
YEAH. ALL THE OTHER KIDS WERE SHOCKED AND UPSET ABOUT GETTING THEIR VOLCANOES STOLEN.
ALL THE OTHER KIDS... ALL THE OTHER KIDS...
SHE'S DOING THAT THINKING THING!
AND SHE'S NOT EVEN WEARING HER THINKING CAP!
BEFORE WE PICK ONE SUSPECT...
WE HAVE TO ELIMINATE ALL THE OTHER POSSIBLE SUSPECTS...
WHICH MEANS WE HAVE TO LOOK AT POSSIBLE MOTIVES.
WHO ELSE HAD A REASON FOR TAKING TWENTY-THREE MODEL VOLCANOES?

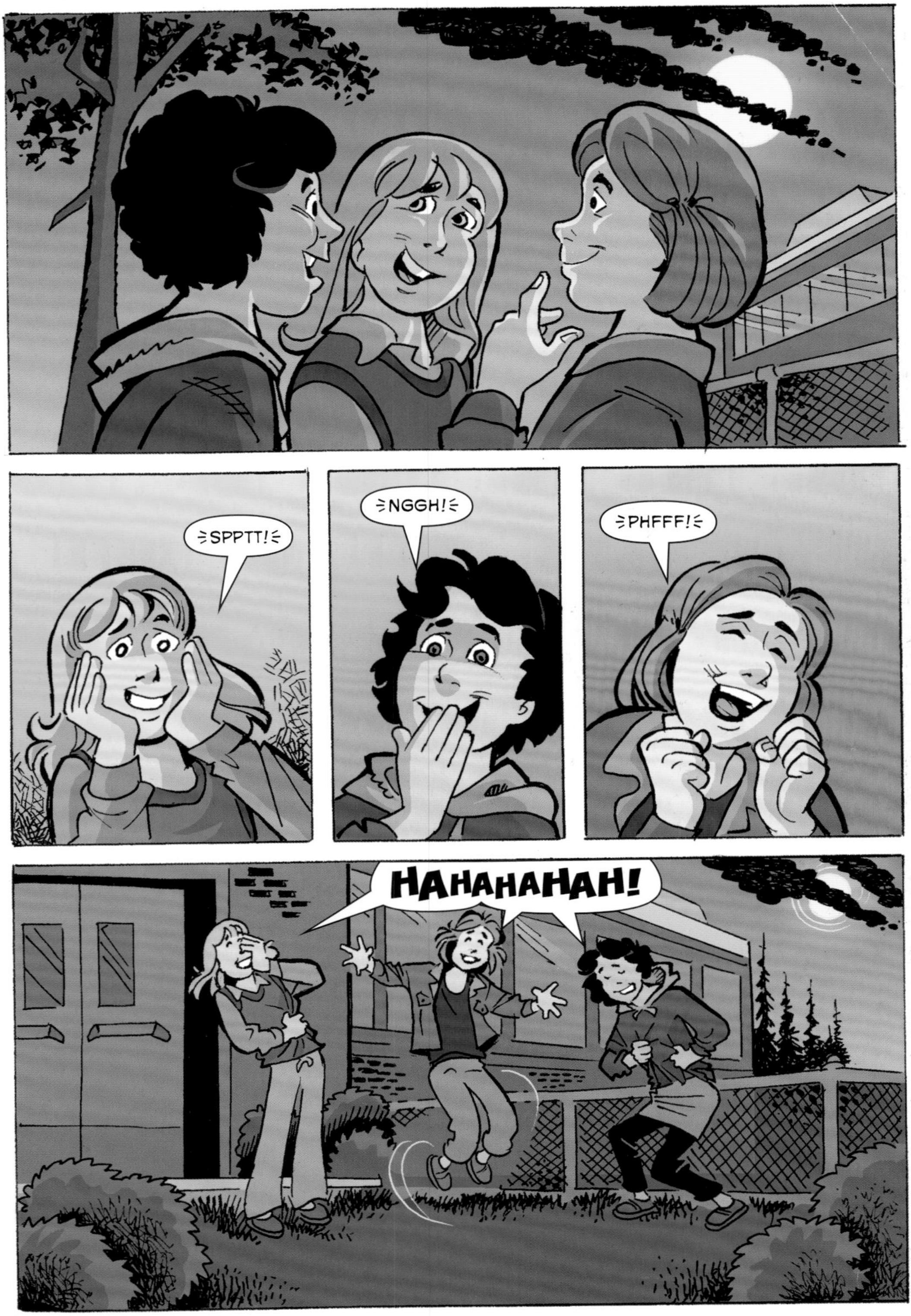
SPPTT!
NGGH!
PHFFF!
HAHAHAHAH!

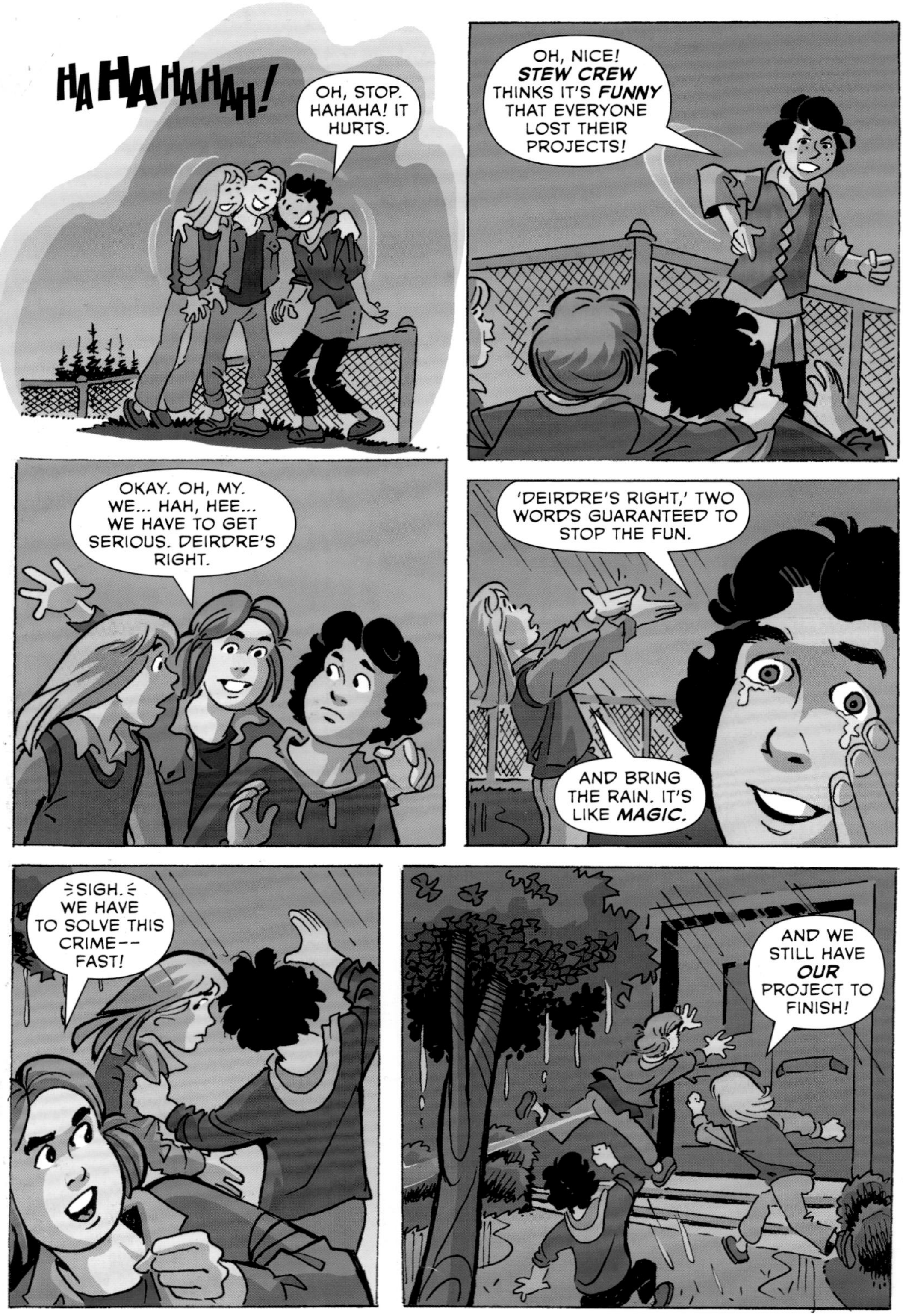

HAHAHAHAH!
OH, STOP. HAHAHA! IT HURTS.
OH, NICE! STEW CREW THINKS IT'S FUNNY THAT EVERYONE LOST THEIR PROJECTS!
OKAY. OH, MY. WE... HAH, HEE... WE HAVE TO GET SERIOUS. DEIRDRE'S RIGHT.
'DEIRDRE'S RIGHT,' TWO WORDS GUARANTEED TO STOP THE FUN.
AND BRING THE RAIN. IT'S LIKE MAGIC.
SIGH. WE HAVE TO SOLVE THIS CRIME-- FAST!
AND WE STILL HAVE OUR PROJECT TO FINISH!

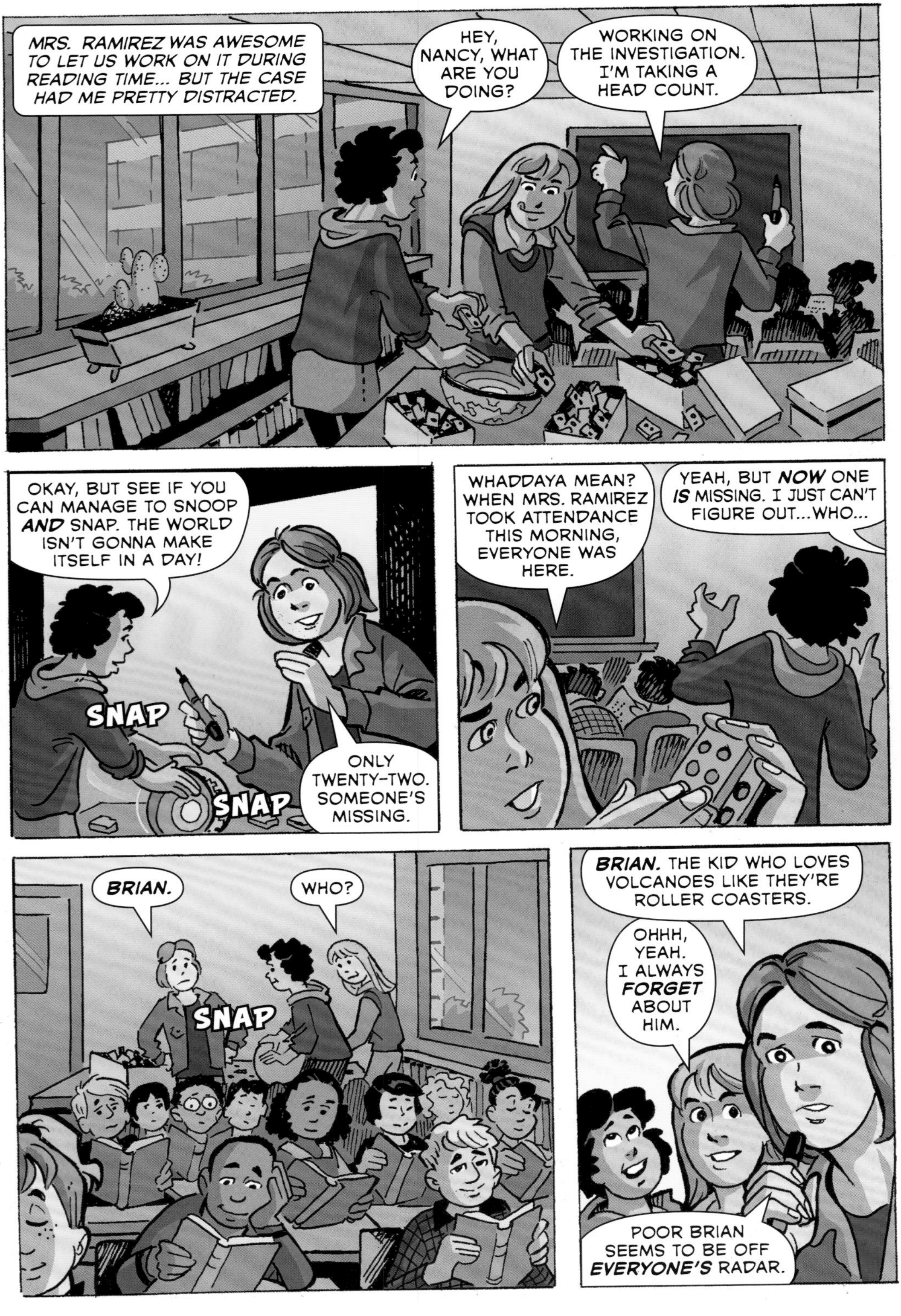

MRS. RAMIREZ WAS AWESOME TO LET US WORK ON IT DURING READING TIME... BUT THE CASE HAD ME PRETTY DISTRACTED.
HEY, NANCY, WHAT ARE YOU DOING?
WORKING ON THE INVESTIGATION. I'M TAKING A HEAD COUNT.
OKAY, BUT SEE IF YOU CAN MANAGE TO SNOOP AND SNAP. THE WORLD ISN'T GONNA MAKE ITSELF IN A DAY!
SNAP
SNAP
ONLY TWENTY-TWO. SOMEONE'S MISSING.
WHADDAYA MEAN? WHEN MRS. RAMIREZ TOOK ATTENDANCE THIS MORNING, EVERYONE WAS HERE.
YEAH, BUT NOW ONE IS MISSING. I JUST CAN'T FIGURE OUT...WHO...
BRIAN.
WHO?
SNAP
BRIAN. THE KID WHO LOVES VOLCANOES LIKE THEY'RE ROLLER COASTERS.
OHHH, YEAH. I ALWAYS FORGET ABOUT HIM.
POOR BRIAN SEEMS TO BE OFF EVERYONE'S RADAR.

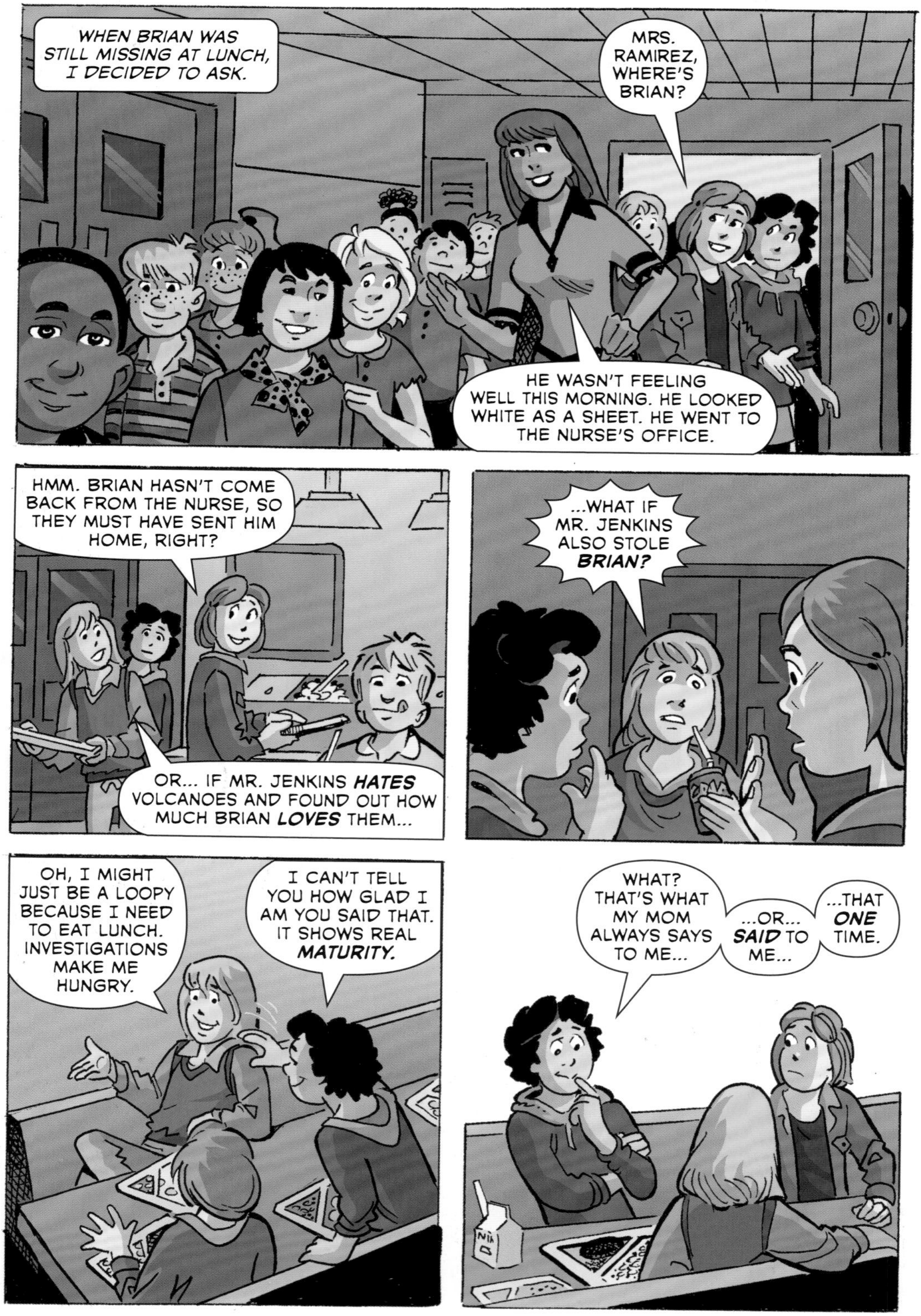
WHEN BRIAN WAS STILL MISSING AT LUNCH, I DECIDED TO ASK.
MRS. RAMIREZ, WHERE'S BRIAN?
HE WASN'T FEELING WELL THIS MORNING. HE LOOKED WHITE AS A SHEET. HE WENT TO THE NURSE'S OFFICE.
HMM. BRIAN HASN'T COME BACK FROM THE NURSE, SO THEY MUST HAVE SENT HIM HOME, RIGHT?
OR... IF MR. JENKINS HATES VOLCANOES AND FOUND OUT HOW MUCH BRIAN LOVES THEM...
...WHAT IF MR. JENKINS ALSO STOLE BRIAN?
OH, I MIGHT JUST BE A LOOPY BECAUSE I NEED TO EAT LUNCH. INVESTIGATIONS MAKE ME HUNGRY.
I CAN'T TELL YOU HOW GLAD I AM YOU SAID THAT. IT SHOWS REAL MATURITY.
WHAT? THAT'S WHAT MY MOM ALWAYS SAYS TO ME...
...OR... SAID TO ME...
...THAT ONE TIME.

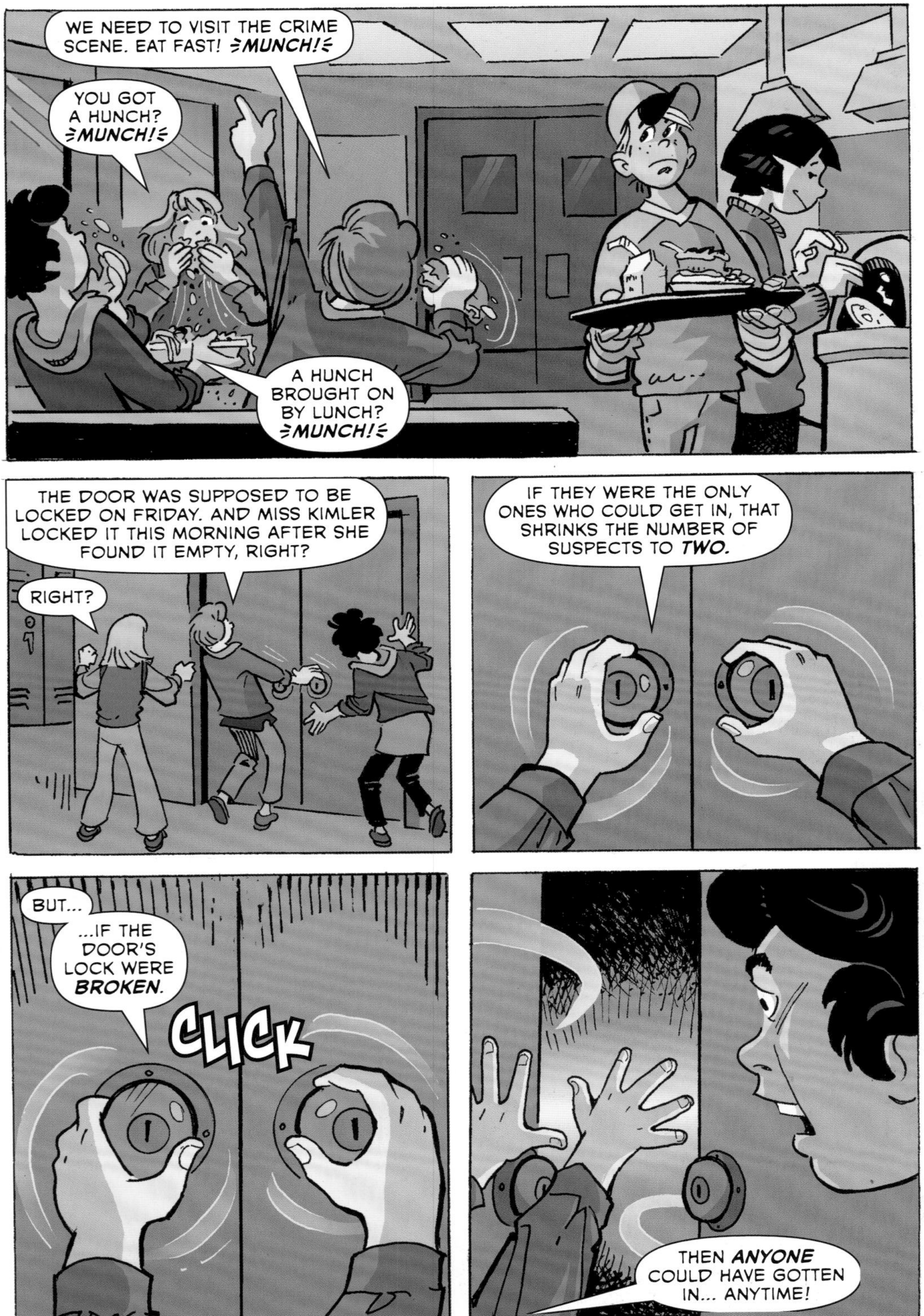
WE NEED TO VISIT THE CRIME SCENE. EAT FAST! MUNCH!
YOU GOT A HUNCH? MUNCH!
A HUNCH BROUGHT ON BY LUNCH? MUNCH!
THE DOOR WAS SUPPOSED TO BE LOCKED ON FRIDAY. AND MISS KIMLER LOCKED IT THIS MORNING AFTER SHE FOUND IT EMPTY, RIGHT?
RIGHT?
IF THEY WERE THE ONLY ONES WHO COULD GET IN, THAT SHRINKS THE NUMBER OF SUSPECTS TO TWO.
BUT...
...IF THE DOOR'S LOCK WERE BROKEN.
CLICK
THEN ANYONE COULD HAVE GOTTEN IN... ANYTIME!

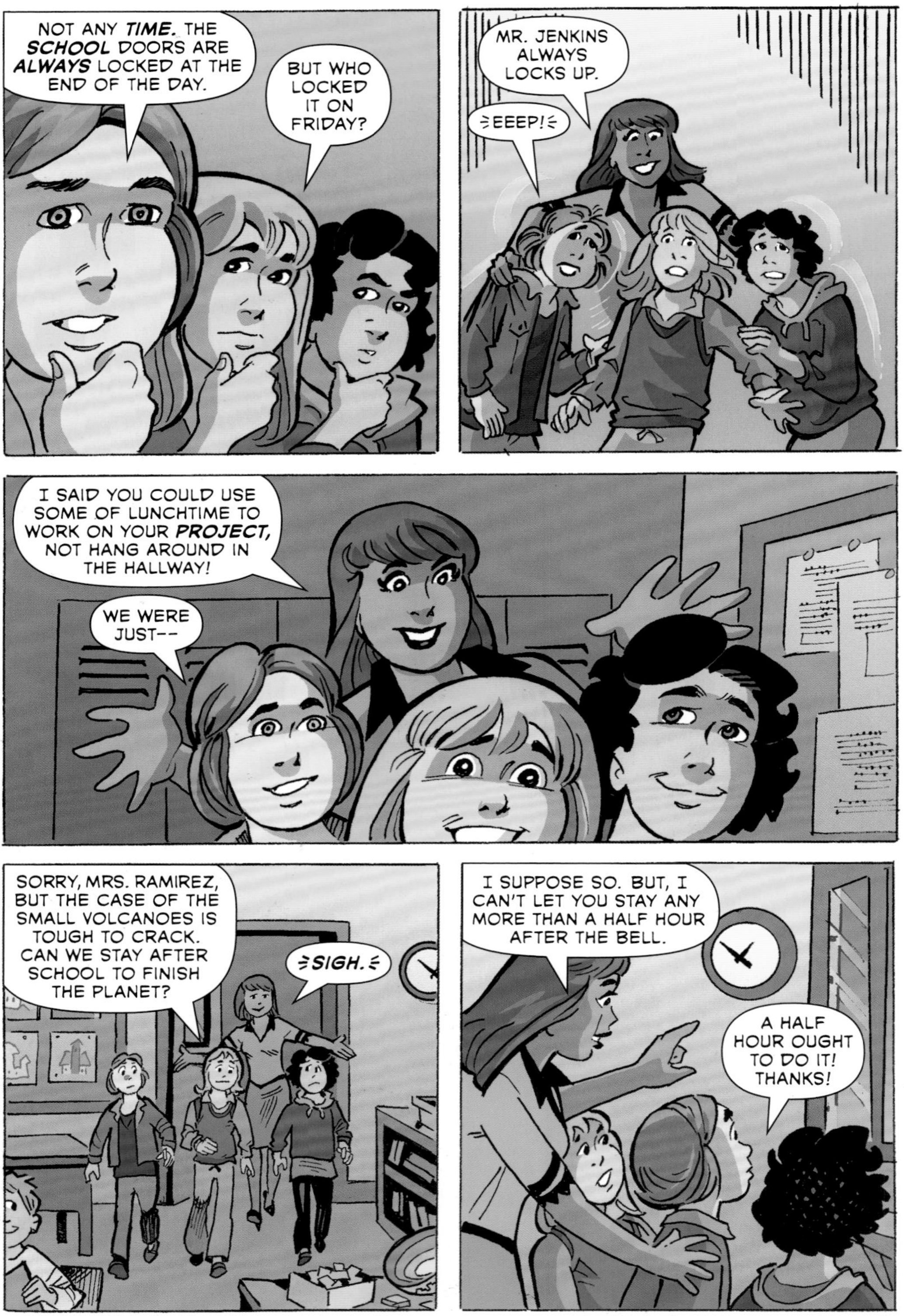
NOT ANY *TIME.* THE *SCHOOL* DOORS ARE *ALWAYS* LOCKED AT THE END OF THE DAY.
BUT WHO LOCKED IT ON FRIDAY?
MR. JENKINS ALWAYS LOCKS UP.
EEEP!
I SAID YOU COULD USE SOME OF LUNCHTIME TO WORK ON YOUR *PROJECT,* NOT HANG AROUND IN THE HALLWAY!
WE WERE JUST--
SORRY, MRS. RAMIREZ, BUT THE CASE OF THE SMALL VOLCANOES IS TOUGH TO CRACK. CAN WE STAY AFTER SCHOOL TO FINISH THE PLANET?
SIGH.
I SUPPOSE SO. BUT, I CAN'T LET YOU STAY ANY MORE THAN A HALF HOUR AFTER THE BELL.
A HALF HOUR OUGHT TO DO IT! THANKS!

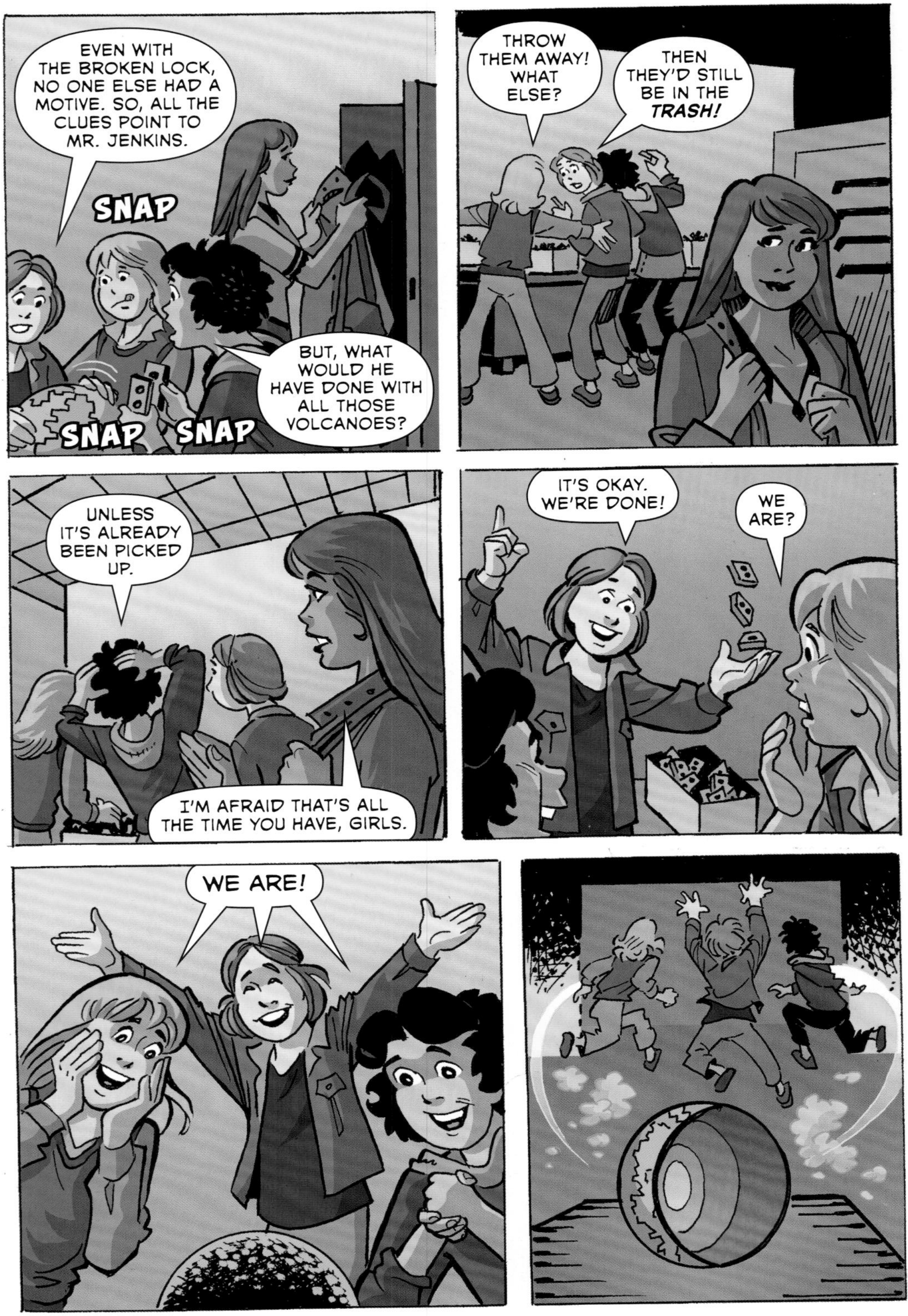
EVEN WITH THE BROKEN LOCK, NO ONE ELSE HAD A MOTIVE. SO, ALL THE CLUES POINT TO MR. JENKINS.
SNAP
BUT, WHAT WOULD HE HAVE DONE WITH ALL THOSE VOLCANOES?
SNAP
SNAP
THROW THEM AWAY! WHAT ELSE?
THEN THEY'D STILL BE IN THE *TRASH!*
UNLESS IT'S ALREADY BEEN PICKED UP.
I'M AFRAID THAT'S ALL THE TIME YOU HAVE, GIRLS.
IT'S OKAY. WE'RE DONE!
WE ARE?
WE ARE!

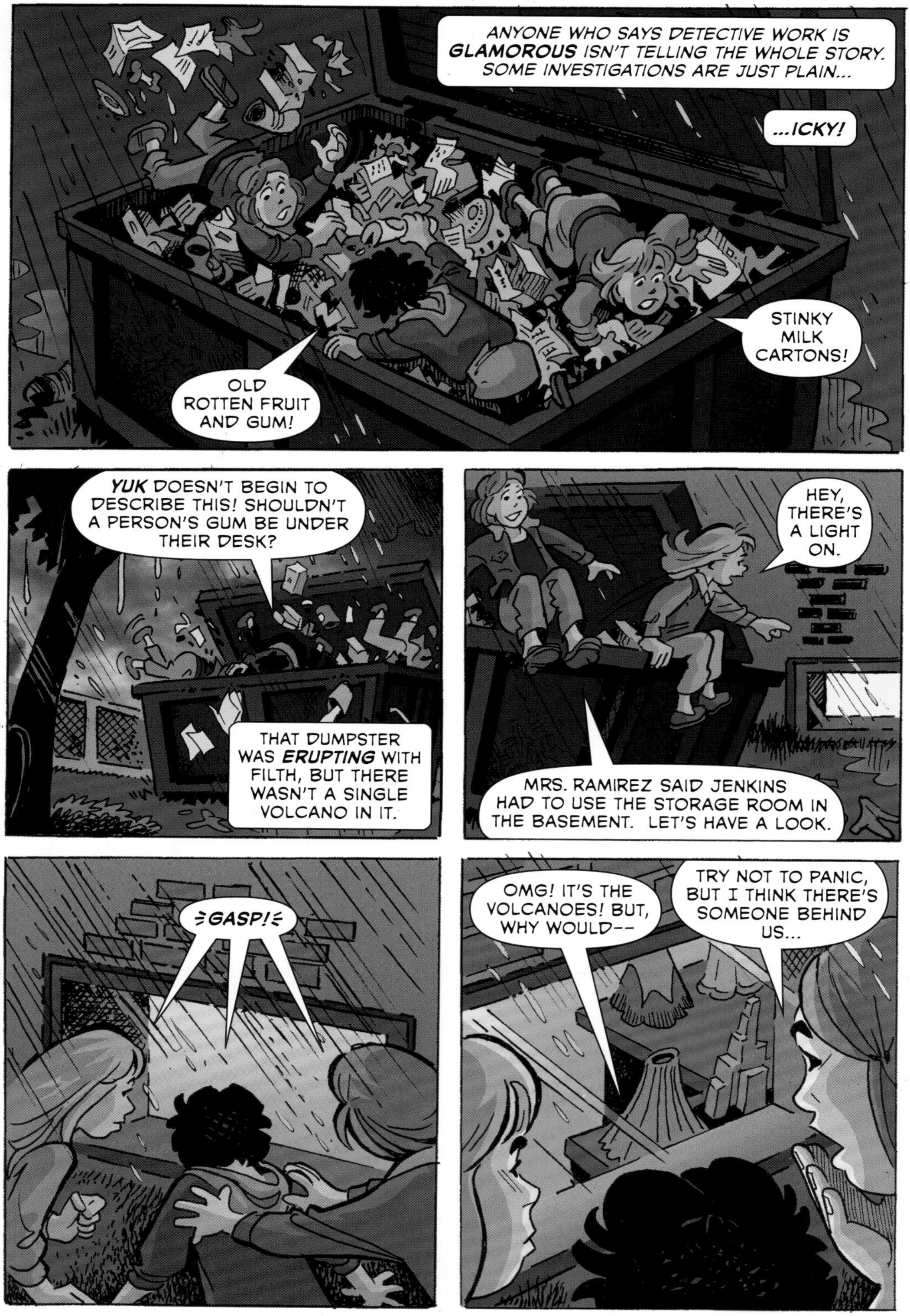
ANYONE WHO SAYS DETECTIVE WORK IS **GLAMOROUS** ISN'T TELLING THE WHOLE STORY. SOME INVESTIGATIONS ARE JUST PLAIN...
...ICKY!
OLD ROTTEN FRUIT AND GUM!
STINKY MILK CARTONS!
YUK DOESN'T BEGIN TO DESCRIBE THIS! SHOULDN'T A PERSON'S GUM BE UNDER THEIR DESK?
THAT DUMPSTER WAS *ERUPTING* WITH FILTH, BUT THERE WASN'T A SINGLE VOLCANO IN IT.
HEY, THERE'S A LIGHT ON.
MRS. RAMIREZ SAID JENKINS HAD TO USE THE STORAGE ROOM IN THE BASEMENT. LET'S HAVE A LOOK.
GASP!
OMG! IT'S THE VOLCANOES! BUT, WHY WOULD--
TRY NOT TO PANIC, BUT I THINK THERE'S SOMEONE BEHIND US...

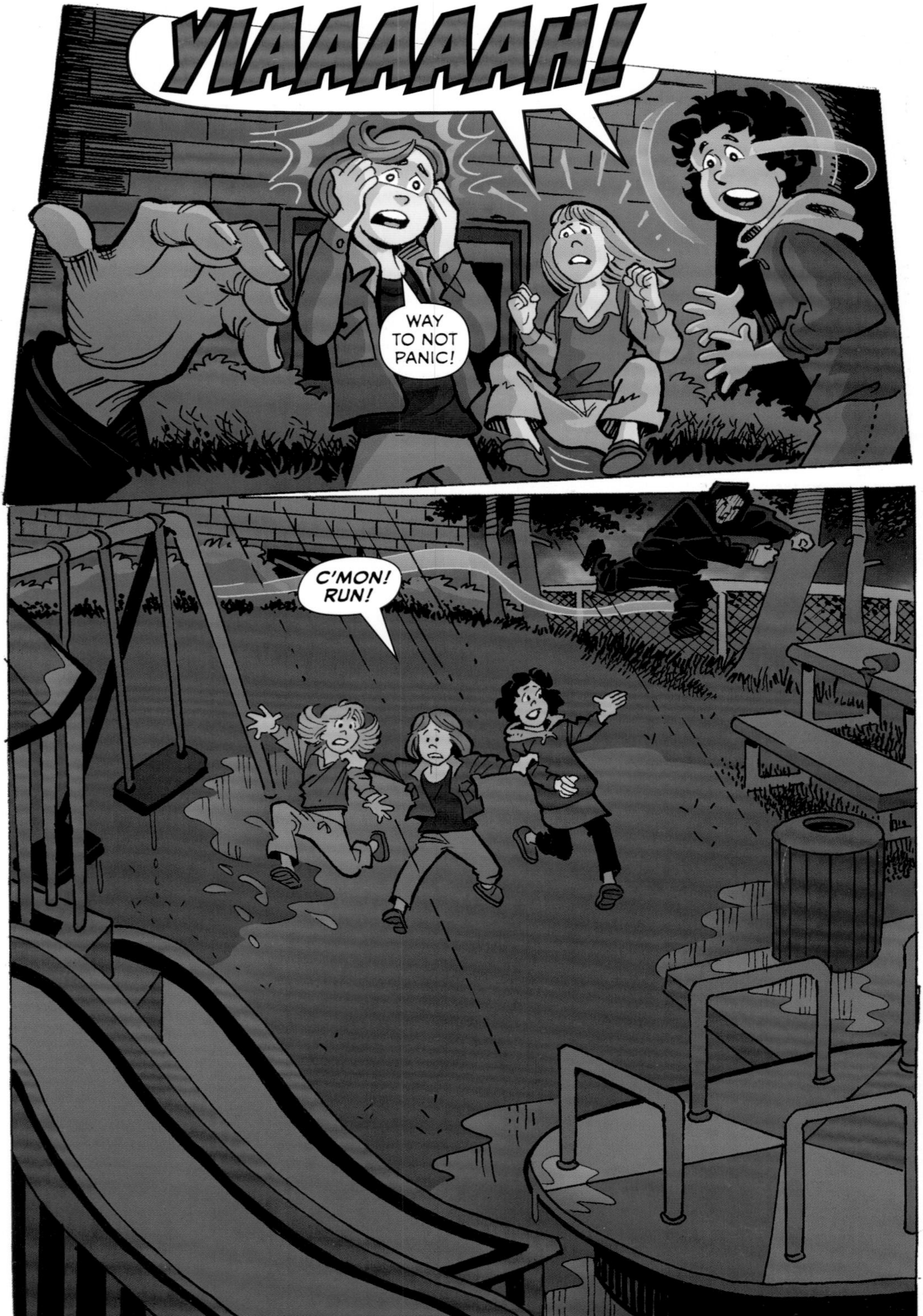
YIAAAAAAH!
WAY TO NOT PANIC!
C'MON! RUN!

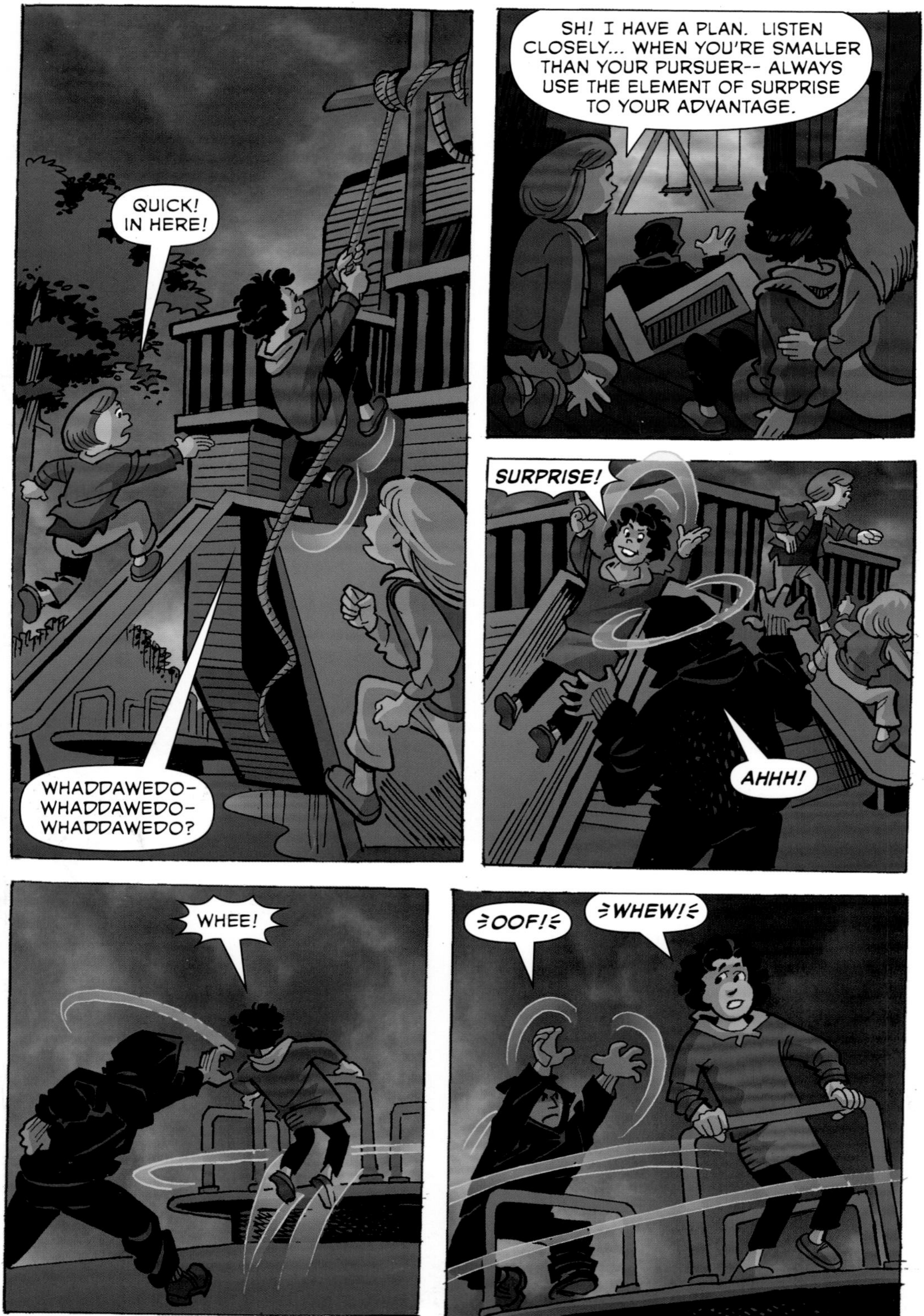
QUICK! IN HERE!
WHADDAWEDO-WHADDAWEDO-WHADDAWEDO?
SH! I HAVE A PLAN. LISTEN CLOSELY... WHEN YOU'RE SMALLER THAN YOUR PURSUER-- ALWAYS USE THE ELEMENT OF SURPRISE TO YOUR ADVANTAGE.
SURPRISE!
AHHH!
WHEE!
OOF!
WHEW!

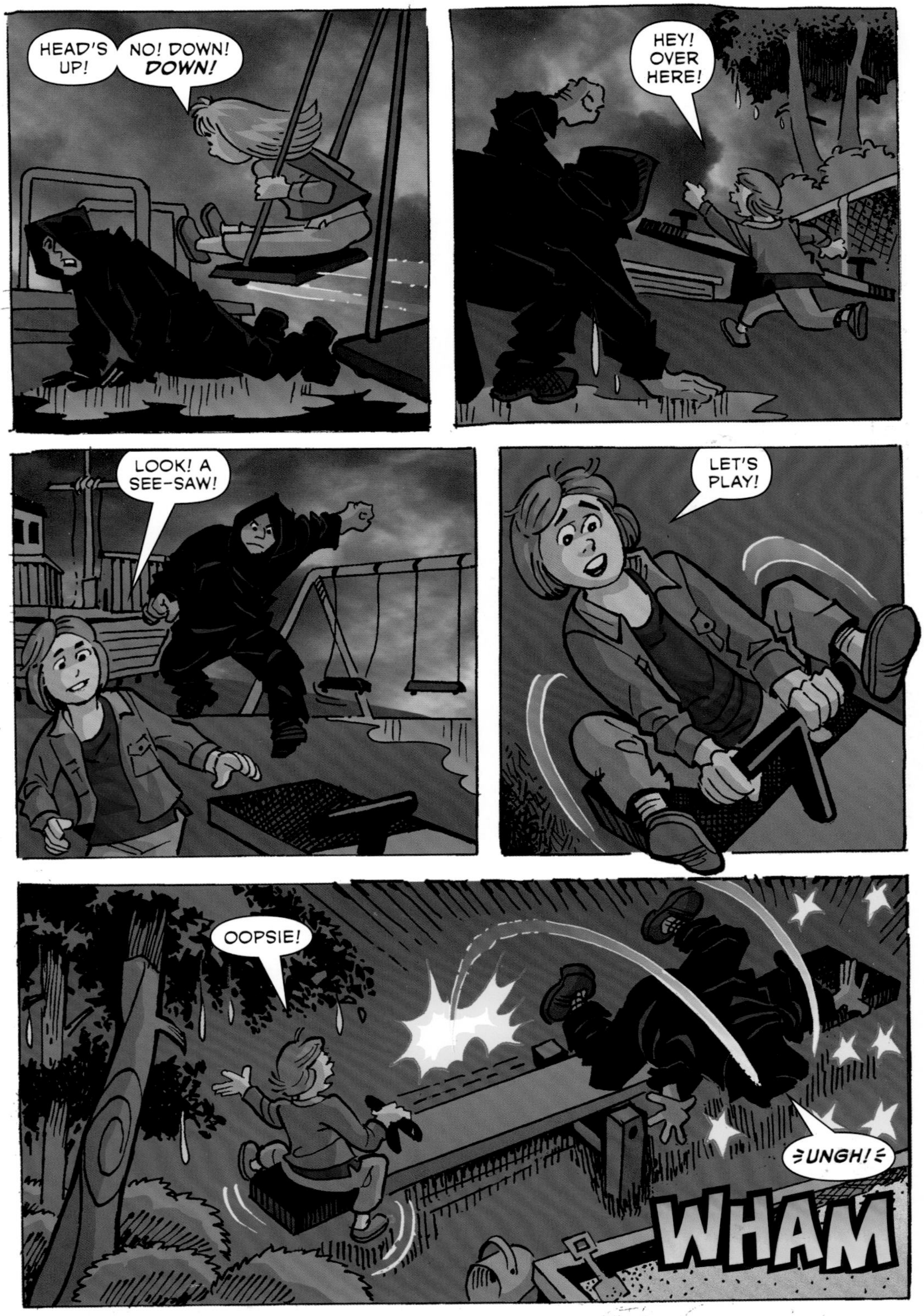
HEAD'S UP!
NO! DOWN! *DOWN!*
HEY! OVER HERE!
LOOK! A SEE-SAW!
LET'S PLAY!
OOPSIE!
UNGH!
WHAM

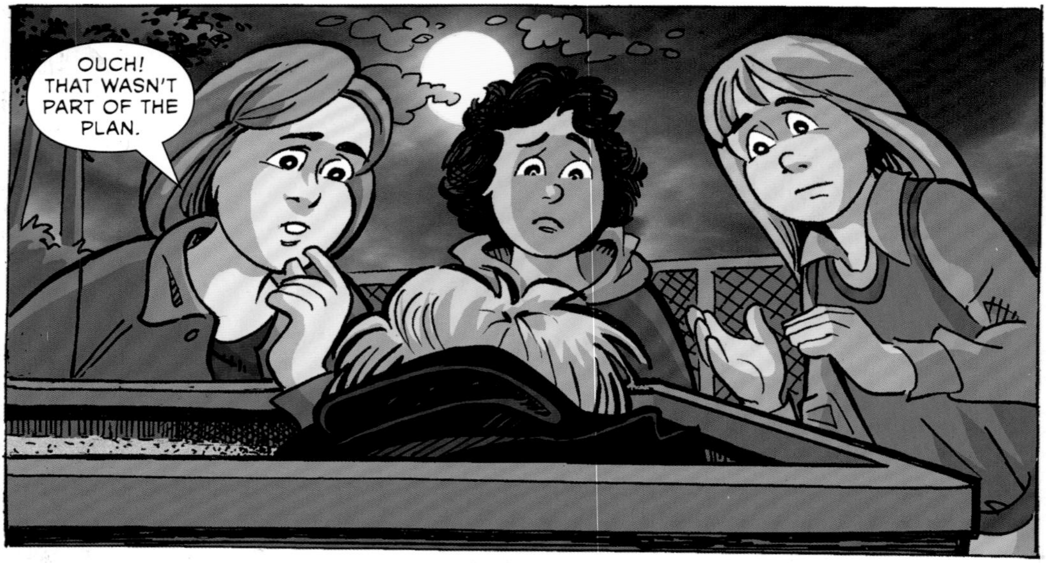
OUCH! THAT WASN'T PART OF THE PLAN.

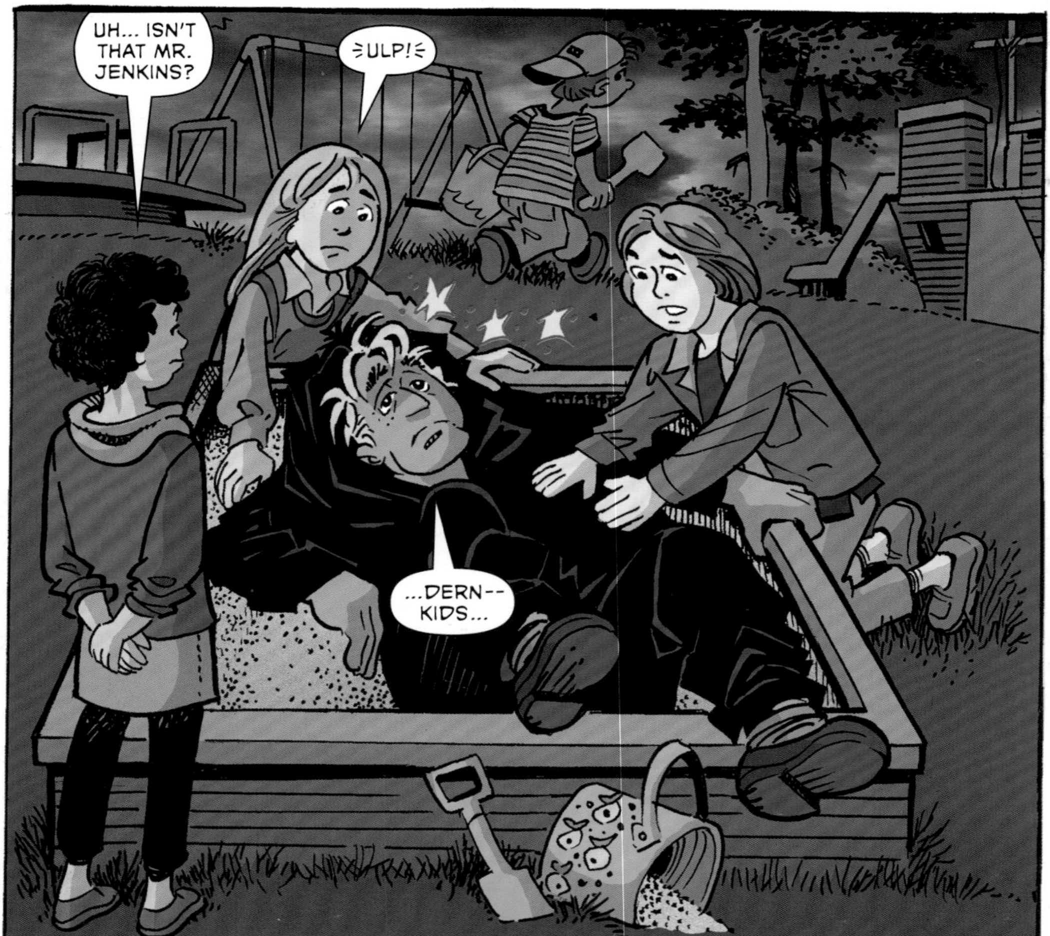
UH... ISN'T THAT MR. JENKINS?
ULP!
...DERN-- KIDS...

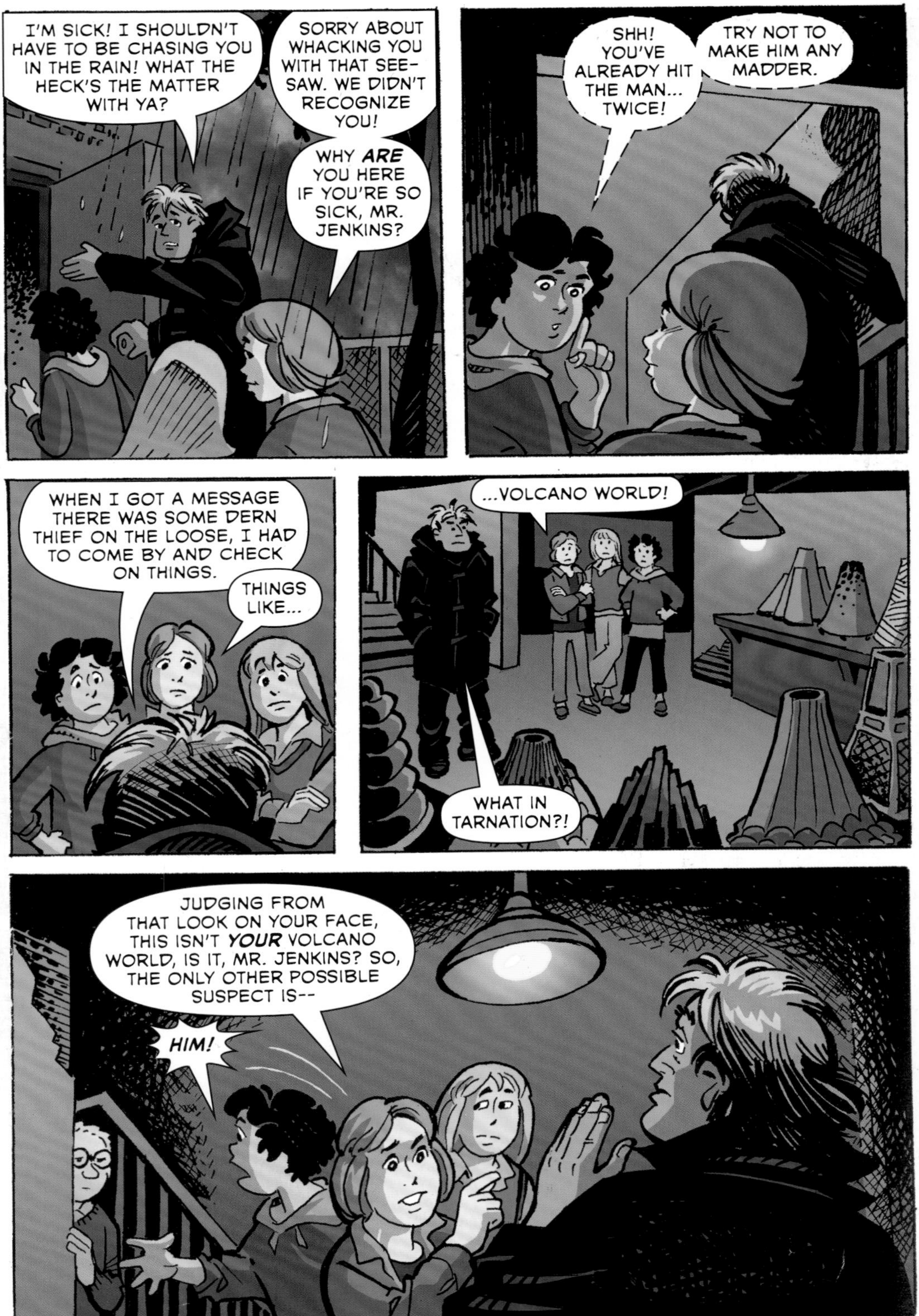
I'M SICK! I SHOULDN'T HAVE TO BE CHASING YOU IN THE RAIN! WHAT THE HECK'S THE MATTER WITH YA?
SORRY ABOUT WHACKING YOU WITH THAT SEE-SAW. WE DIDN'T RECOGNIZE YOU!
WHY **ARE** YOU HERE IF YOU'RE SO SICK, MR. JENKINS?
SHH! YOU'VE ALREADY HIT THE MAN... TWICE!
TRY NOT TO MAKE HIM ANY MADDER.
WHEN I GOT A MESSAGE THERE WAS SOME DERN THIEF ON THE LOOSE, I HAD TO COME BY AND CHECK ON THINGS.
THINGS LIKE...
...VOLCANO WORLD!
WHAT IN TARNATION?!
JUDGING FROM THAT LOOK ON YOUR FACE, THIS ISN'T **YOUR** VOLCANO WORLD, IS IT, MR. JENKINS? SO, THE ONLY OTHER POSSIBLE SUSPECT IS--
HIM!

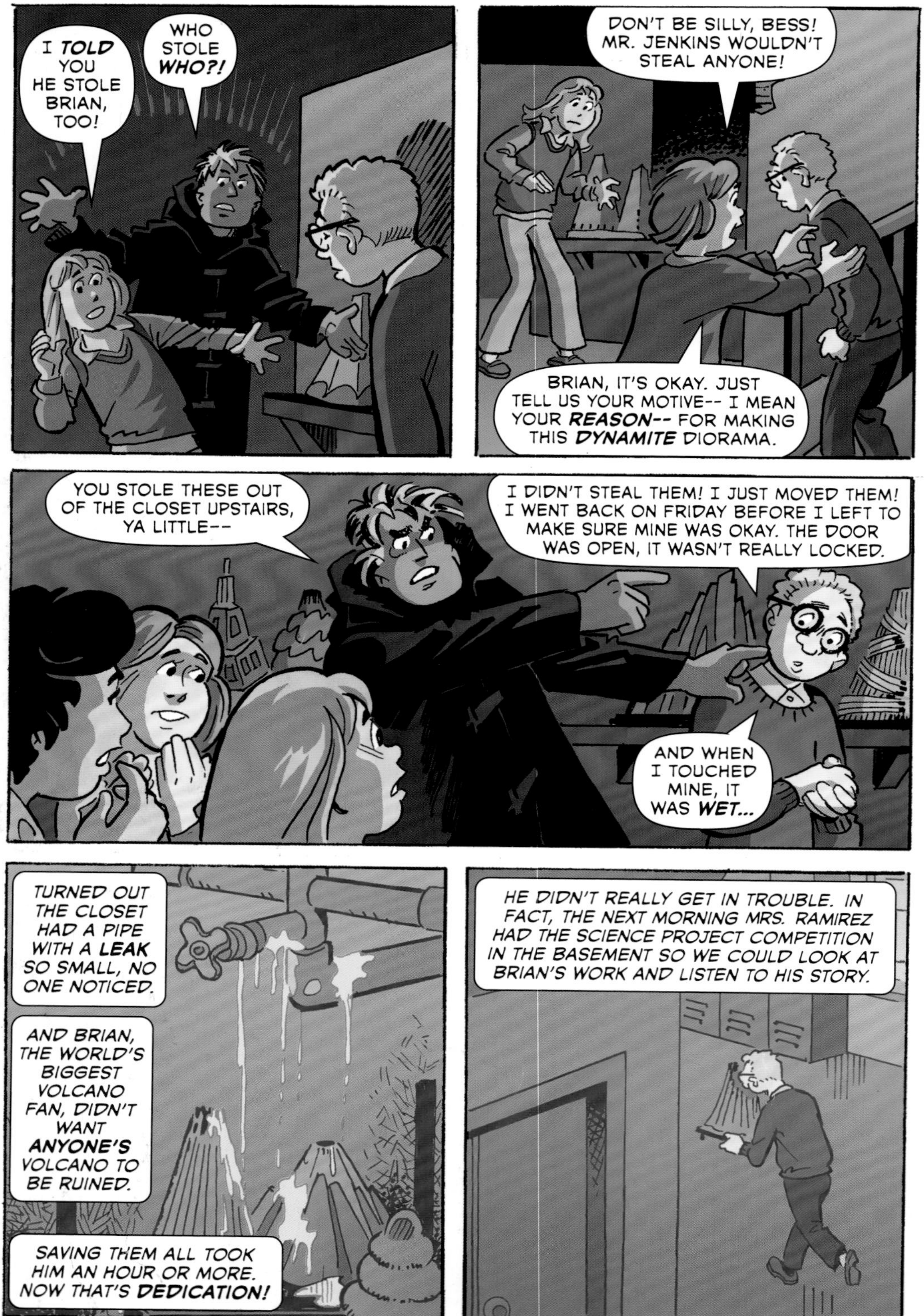
I TOLD YOU HE STOLE BRIAN, TOO!
WHO STOLE WHO?!
DON'T BE SILLY, BESS! MR. JENKINS WOULDN'T STEAL ANYONE!
BRIAN, IT'S OKAY. JUST TELL US YOUR MOTIVE-- I MEAN YOUR REASON-- FOR MAKING THIS DYNAMITE DIORAMA.
YOU STOLE THESE OUT OF THE CLOSET UPSTAIRS, YA LITTLE--
I DIDN'T STEAL THEM! I JUST MOVED THEM! I WENT BACK ON FRIDAY BEFORE I LEFT TO MAKE SURE MINE WAS OKAY. THE DOOR WAS OPEN, IT WASN'T REALLY LOCKED.
AND WHEN I TOUCHED MINE, IT WAS WET...
TURNED OUT THE CLOSET HAD A PIPE WITH A LEAK SO SMALL, NO ONE NOTICED.
AND BRIAN, THE WORLD'S BIGGEST VOLCANO FAN, DIDN'T WANT ANYONE'S VOLCANO TO BE RUINED.
SAVING THEM ALL TOOK HIM AN HOUR OR MORE. NOW THAT'S DEDICATION!
HE DIDN'T REALLY GET IN TROUBLE. IN FACT, THE NEXT MORNING MRS. RAMIREZ HAD THE SCIENCE PROJECT COMPETITION IN THE BASEMENT SO WE COULD LOOK AT BRIAN'S WORK AND LISTEN TO HIS STORY.

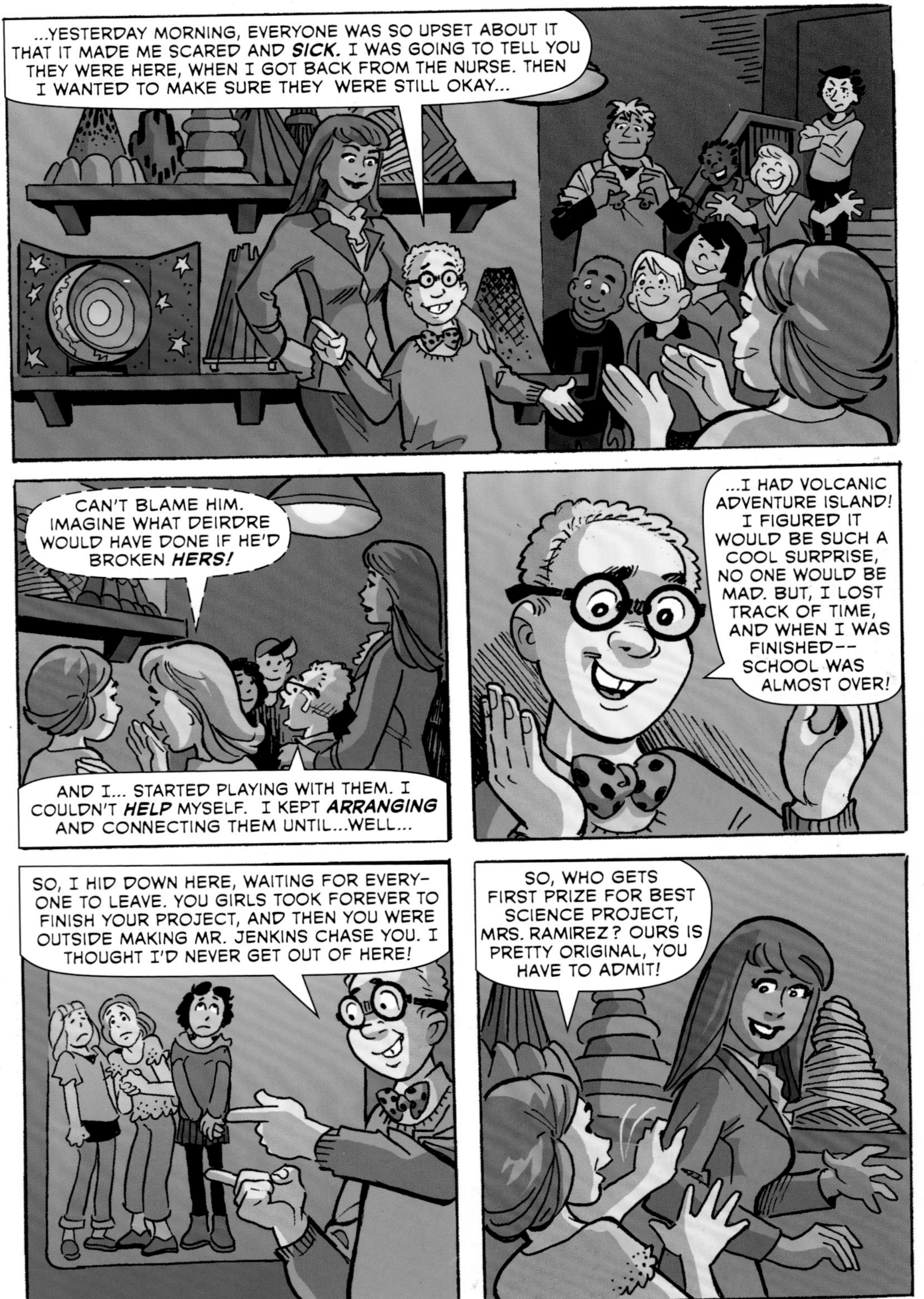
...YESTERDAY MORNING, EVERYONE WAS SO UPSET ABOUT IT THAT IT MADE ME SCARED AND SICK. I WAS GOING TO TELL YOU THEY WERE HERE, WHEN I GOT BACK FROM THE NURSE. THEN I WANTED TO MAKE SURE THEY WERE STILL OKAY...
CAN'T BLAME HIM. IMAGINE WHAT DEIRDRE WOULD HAVE DONE IF HE'D BROKEN HERS!
AND I... STARTED PLAYING WITH THEM. I COULDN'T HELP MYSELF. I KEPT ARRANGING AND CONNECTING THEM UNTIL...WELL...
...I HAD VOLCANIC ADVENTURE ISLAND! I FIGURED IT WOULD BE SUCH A COOL SURPRISE, NO ONE WOULD BE MAD. BUT, I LOST TRACK OF TIME, AND WHEN I WAS FINISHED-- SCHOOL WAS ALMOST OVER!
SO, I HID DOWN HERE, WAITING FOR EVERY-ONE TO LEAVE. YOU GIRLS TOOK FOREVER TO FINISH YOUR PROJECT, AND THEN YOU WERE OUTSIDE MAKING MR. JENKINS CHASE YOU. I THOUGHT I'D NEVER GET OUT OF HERE!
SO, WHO GETS FIRST PRIZE FOR BEST SCIENCE PROJECT, MRS. RAMIREZ? OURS IS PRETTY ORIGINAL, YOU HAVE TO ADMIT!

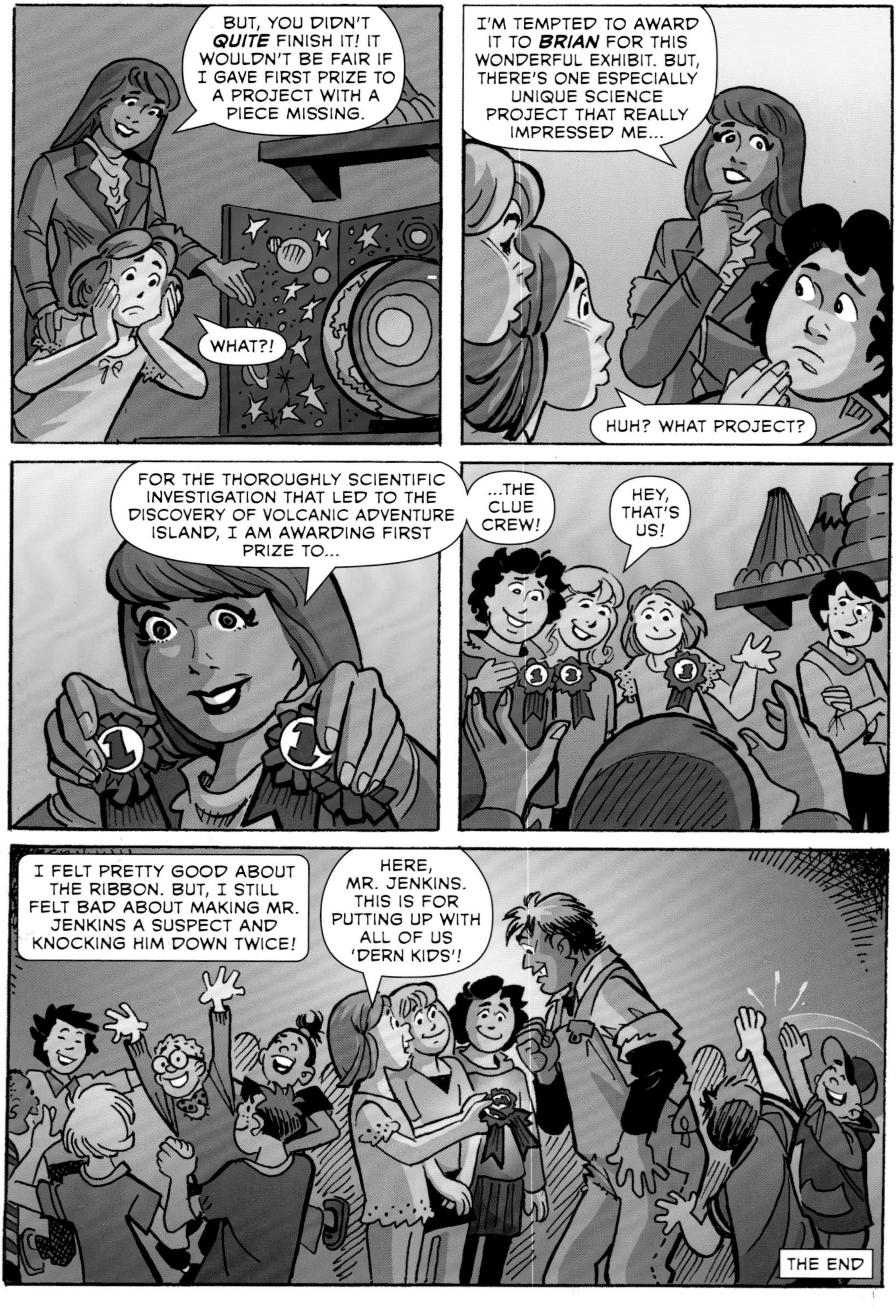
BUT, YOU DIDN'T QUITE FINISH IT! IT WOULDN'T BE FAIR IF I GAVE FIRST PRIZE TO A PROJECT WITH A PIECE MISSING.
WHAT?!
I'M TEMPTED TO AWARD IT TO BRIAN FOR THIS WONDERFUL EXHIBIT. BUT, THERE'S ONE ESPECIALLY UNIQUE SCIENCE PROJECT THAT REALLY IMPRESSED ME...
HUH? WHAT PROJECT?
FOR THE THOROUGHLY SCIENTIFIC INVESTIGATION THAT LED TO THE DISCOVERY OF VOLCANIC ADVENTURE ISLAND, I AM AWARDING FIRST PRIZE TO...
...THE CLUE CREW!
HEY, THAT'S US!
I FELT PRETTY GOOD ABOUT THE RIBBON. BUT, I STILL FELT BAD ABOUT MAKING MR. JENKINS A SUSPECT AND KNOCKING HIM DOWN TWICE!
HERE, MR. JENKINS. THIS IS FOR PUTTING UP WITH ALL OF US 'DERN KIDS'!
THE END

WATCH OUT FOR PAPERCUTZ

NANCY DREW MYSTERY STORIES
THE SECRET OF THE OLD CLOCK
by CAROLYN KEENE

Welcome to the felicitous first NANCY DREW AND THE CLUE CREW graphic novel from your friends at Papercutz, the folks dedicated to publishing great graphic novels for all ages. I'm Jim Salicrup, Editor-in Chief and former Teen Sleuth, here to provide little background on the world's greatest Girl Detective and what else is new at Papercutz.

In 1930 the first four Nancy Drew novels appeared under the byline of Carolyne Keene and were an instant publishing phenomenon. The idea was simple—a young female detective who could out-smart any adversary! Since then there have been a gazillion NANCY DREW MYSTERY STORIES, movies, television series, computer games, and much, much more. Nancy's exploits have inspired such women as Supreme Court Justices Sandra Day O'Connor and Sonia Sotomayor, Secretary of State Hillary Rodham Clinton, and former First Lady Laura Bush.

NEW STORY! FULL-COLOR GRAPHIC NOVEL
NANCY DREW
girl detective
#1
The Demon of River Heights
BASED ON THE SERIES BY CAROLYN KEENE
Stefan PETRUCHA • Vaughn ROSS
PAPERCUTZ

But it wasn't until 2005, when Papercutz launched the NANCY DREW Girl Detective graphic novels, that she appeared in comics for the first time. There are over 24 NANCY DREW graphic novels, and now there's NANCY DREW AND THE CLUE CREW #1 "Small Volcanoes." The story's by Stefan Petrucha and Sarah Kinney, who have written most of the NANCY DREW graphic novels, and it's illustrated by Stan Goldberg, recent winner of the National Cartoonists Society Gold Key Hall of Fame Award. Stan has been the top artist at Archie Comics for many years and we're all thrilled to have him illustrating NANCY DREW, not to mention THE THREE STOOGES as well, at Papercutz.

As excited as we are about Nancy's latest, and perhaps greatest graphic novel series yet, there's all sorts of other exciting events happening at Papercutz as well! Not only are we continuing to publish the best-selling GERONIMO STILTON graphic novels, we're pleased to announce we'll be adding an all-new spin-off series, entitled THEA STILTON. Now, even Nancy Drew would assume the series would be all about Geronimo's adventurous sister, Thea Stilton, but she'd be mistaken! The THEA STILTON graphic novels star the Thea Sisters, who are five fun students at Mouseford Academy on Whale Island, who want to be journalists just like their hero, Thea Stilton! Check out the special preview on the following pages to get an idea how fabulous this new series will be!

All-new full-color Graphic Novel
Thea Stilton
THE SECRET OF WHALE ISLAND

But that's not all, as a special holiday treat for Papercutz fans everywhere, CLASSICS ILLUSTRATED DELUXE #9 "Scrooge" features beautiful adaptations of Charles Dickens's "A Christmas Carol" and "A Remembrance of Mugby." Check out the preview by writer Rodolphe and artist Estelle Meyrand on the following pages.

Most importantly, let us know what you think of NANCY DREW AND THE CLUE CREW #1! You can reach us at the contacts listed below. So, until we meet again in NANCY DREW AND THE CLUE CREW #2 "Secret Sand Sleuths," this is Jim Salicrup, boy editor signing off!

Jim

FULL-COLOR GRAPHIC NOVEL ADAPTATION
CLASSICS Illustrated Deluxe
A Christmas Carol & The Remembrance of Mugby
Scrooge
by Charles Dickens
Adapted by Rodolphe & Estelle Meyrand
PAPERCUTZ

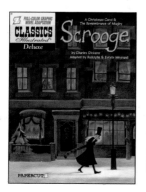

STAY IN TOUCH!

EMAIL:	salicrup@papercutz.com
WEB:	www.papercutz.com
TWITTER:	@papercutzgn
FACEBOOK:	PAPERCUTZGRAPHICNOVELS
BIRTHDAY CARDS:	Papercutz, 160 Broadway, Suite 700, east Wing, New York, NY 100038

Special preview of THEA STILTON Graphic Novel #1 "The Secret of Whale Island"!

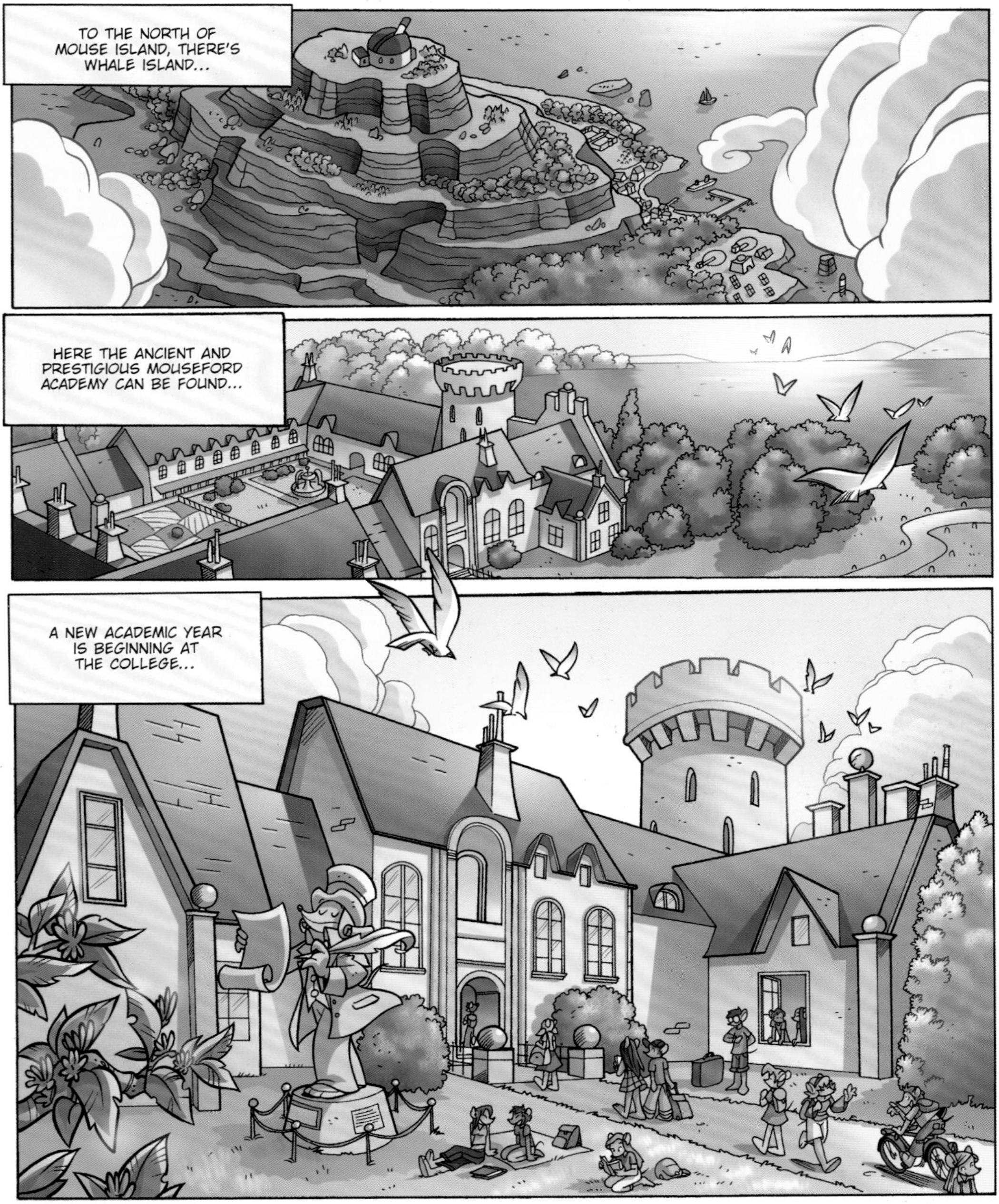
TO THE NORTH OF MOUSE ISLAND, THERE'S WHALE ISLAND...
HERE THE ANCIENT AND PRESTIGIOUS MOUSEFORD ACADEMY CAN BE FOUND...
A NEW ACADEMIC YEAR IS BEGINNING AT THE COLLEGE...

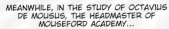

ACCORDING TO TRADITION, THE START OF COLLEGE CLASSES COINCIDES WITH THE ARRIVAL OF THE WHALES IN THE SEAS AROUND THE ISLAND...

BUT WHEN DO THEY ARRIVE, GRANDPA?

IN A FEW DAYS YOU WILL SEE THEM, MARINA!

UNLESS THAT *MYSTERIOUS ORCA* DID NOT MAKE THEM CHANGE COURSE!

MEANWHILE, IN THE STUDY OF OCTAVIUS DE MOUSUS, THE HEADMASTER OF MOUSEFORD ACADEMY...

CALAMITOUS CATS AND SASSAFRAS RATS! YOU CAN'T BE SERIOUS, THEA? YOU CAN'T MISS THE START OF THE ACADEMIC YEAR! WE CAN'T HOLD THE BIG DANCE WITHOUT YOU HERE!

CALM DOWN! I WILL DO EVERYTHING I CAN TO ARRIVE IN TIME FOR THE PROM, I PROMISE! SO, WHAT ARE THE THEA SISTERS UP TO?

WELL DONE! YOU CAN REST EASY, DEAR HEADMASTER.

THEY VOLUNTEERED TO ORGANIZE THE PARTY! THEY HAVE A SOFT SPOT FOR IMPOSSIBLE MISSIONS... AND I TRUST THEM!

I WOULD, IF I COULD... BUT EVERY YEAR IS A NEW YEAR, THEA! AND EVERY NEW YEAR ALWAYS BRINGS SOMETHING NEW!

IT'LL BE BEAUTIFUL, YOU'LL SEE!

ONE THING'S FOR SURE! REMEMBER SARDINIA SQUID? DINA? SHE WON A SCHOLARSHIP TO MOUSEFORD!

"DINA HAS DONE IT! SHE'LL BE THE FIRST WHALE ISLAND RESIDENT TO ATTEND MOUSEFORD!"

MY BABY! →SNIFF←

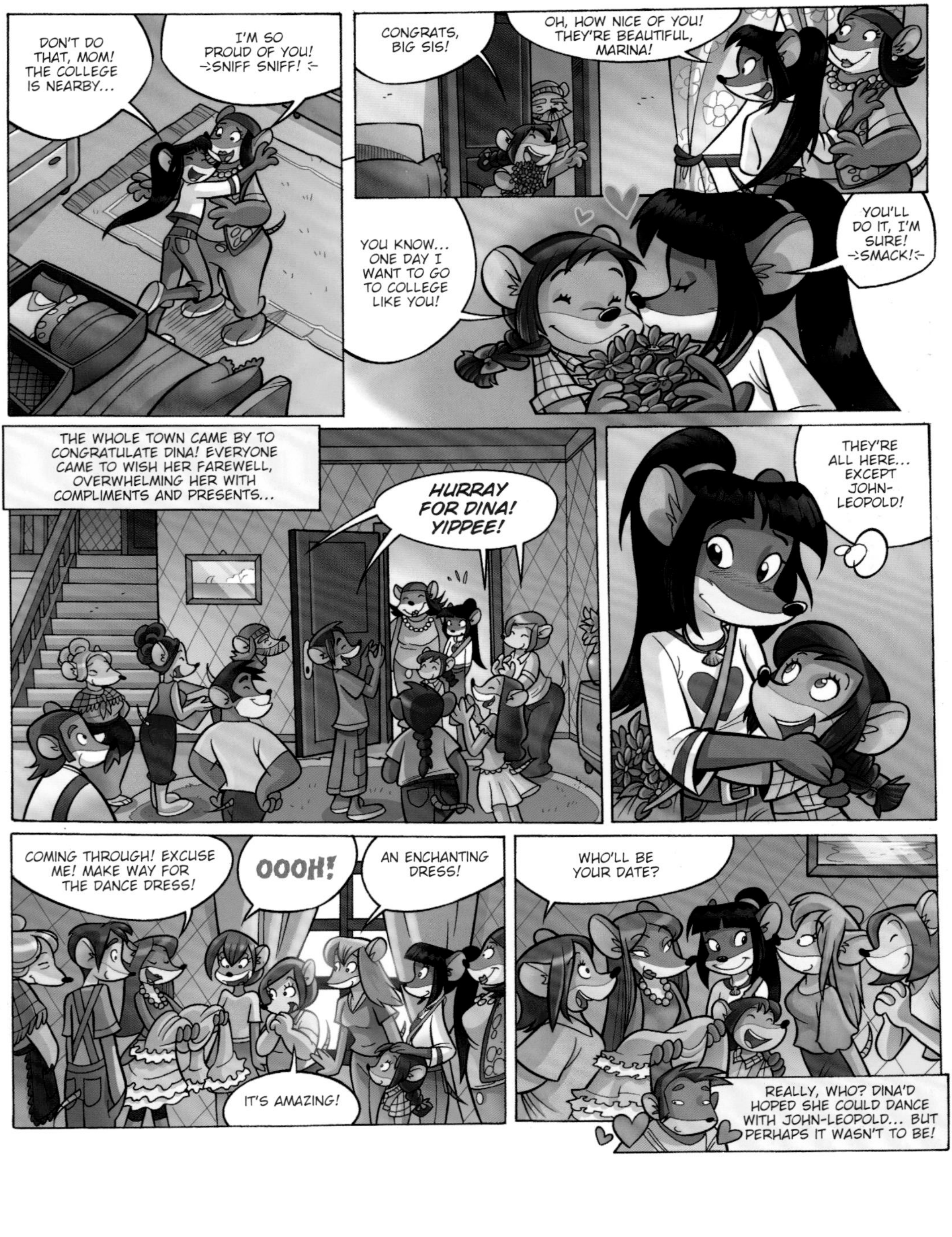
DON'T DO THAT, MOM! THE COLLEGE IS NEARBY...
I'M SO PROUD OF YOU! -SNIFF SNIFF!-
CONGRATS, BIG SIS!
OH, HOW NICE OF YOU! THEY'RE BEAUTIFUL, MARINA!
YOU KNOW... ONE DAY I WANT TO GO TO COLLEGE LIKE YOU!
YOU'LL DO IT, I'M SURE! -SMACK!-
THE WHOLE TOWN CAME BY TO CONGRATULATE DINA! EVERYONE CAME TO WISH HER FAREWELL, OVERWHELMING HER WITH COMPLIMENTS AND PRESENTS...
HURRAY FOR DINA! YIPPEE!
THEY'RE ALL HERE... EXCEPT JOHN-LEOPOLD!
COMING THROUGH! EXCUSE ME! MAKE WAY FOR THE DANCE DRESS!
OOOH!
AN ENCHANTING DRESS!
IT'S AMAZING!
WHO'LL BE YOUR DATE?
REALLY, WHO? DINA'D HOPED SHE COULD DANCE WITH JOHN-LEOPOLD... BUT PERHAPS IT WASN'T TO BE!

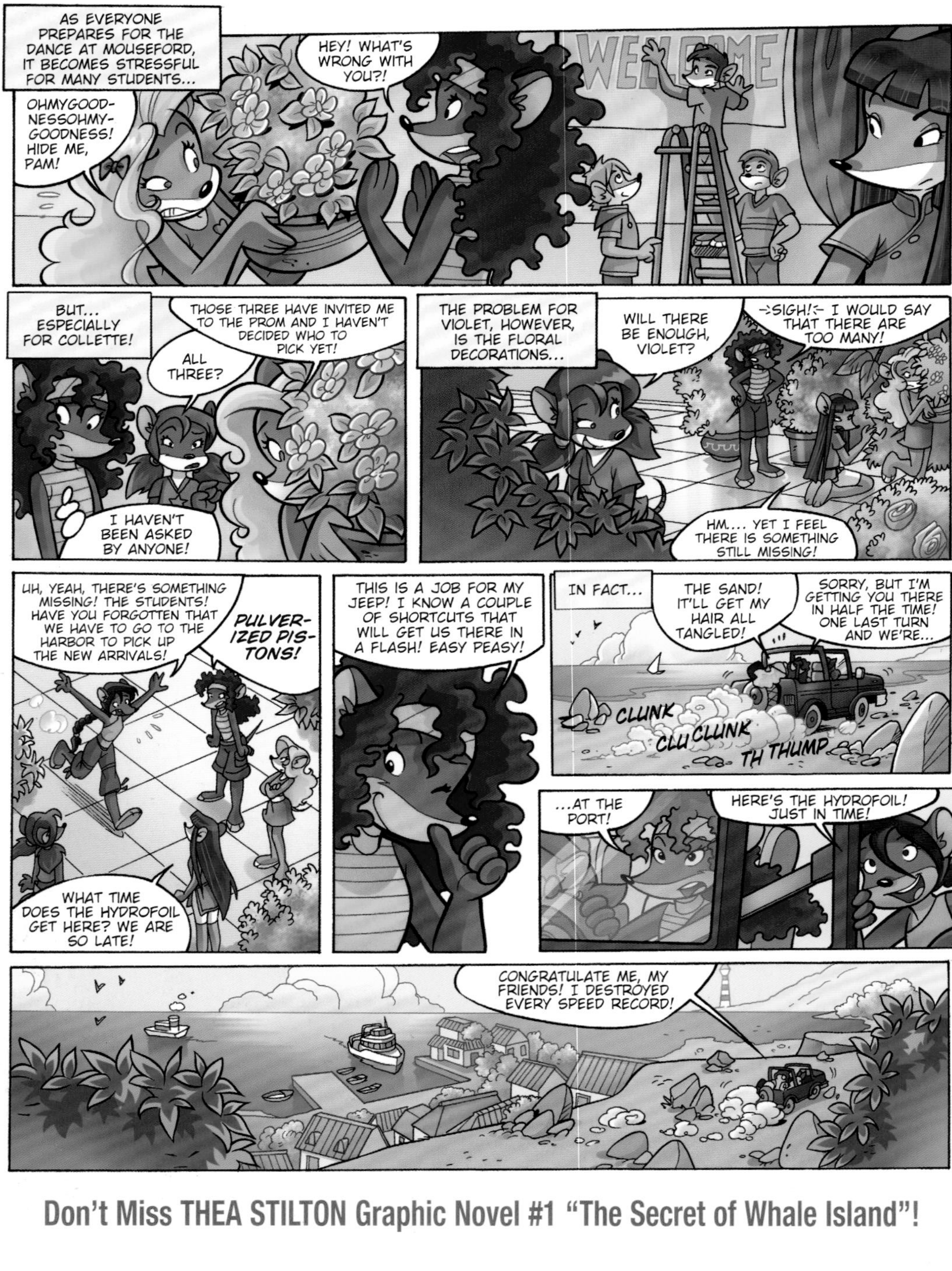
AS EVERYONE PREPARES FOR THE DANCE AT MOUSEFORD, IT BECOMES STRESSFUL FOR MANY STUDENTS...
OHMYGOODNESSOHMYGOODNESS! HIDE ME, PAM!
HEY! WHAT'S WRONG WITH YOU?!
WELCOME
BUT... ESPECIALLY FOR COLLETTE!
THOSE THREE HAVE INVITED ME TO THE PROM AND I HAVEN'T DECIDED WHO TO PICK YET!
ALL THREE?
I HAVEN'T BEEN ASKED BY ANYONE!
THE PROBLEM FOR VIOLET, HOWEVER, IS THE FLORAL DECORATIONS...
WILL THERE BE ENOUGH, VIOLET?
-SIGH!- I WOULD SAY THAT THERE ARE TOO MANY!
HM... YET I FEEL THERE IS SOMETHING STILL MISSING!
UH, YEAH, THERE'S SOMETHING MISSING! THE STUDENTS! HAVE YOU FORGOTTEN THAT WE HAVE TO GO TO THE HARBOR TO PICK UP THE NEW ARRIVALS!
PULVERIZED PISTONS!
WHAT TIME DOES THE HYDROFOIL GET HERE? WE ARE SO LATE!
THIS IS A JOB FOR MY JEEP! I KNOW A COUPLE OF SHORTCUTS THAT WILL GET US THERE IN A FLASH! EASY PEASY!
IN FACT...
THE SAND! IT'LL GET MY HAIR ALL TANGLED!
SORRY, BUT I'M GETTING YOU THERE IN HALF THE TIME! ONE LAST TURN AND WE'RE...
CLUNK
CLU CLUNK
TH THUMP
...AT THE PORT!
HERE'S THE HYDROFOIL! JUST IN TIME!
CONGRATULATE ME, MY FRIENDS! I DESTROYED EVERY SPEED RECORD!

Don't Miss THEA STILTON Graphic Novel #1 "The Secret of Whale Island"!

Special Preview from CLASSICS ILLUSTRATED DELUXE #9 "Scrooge"...

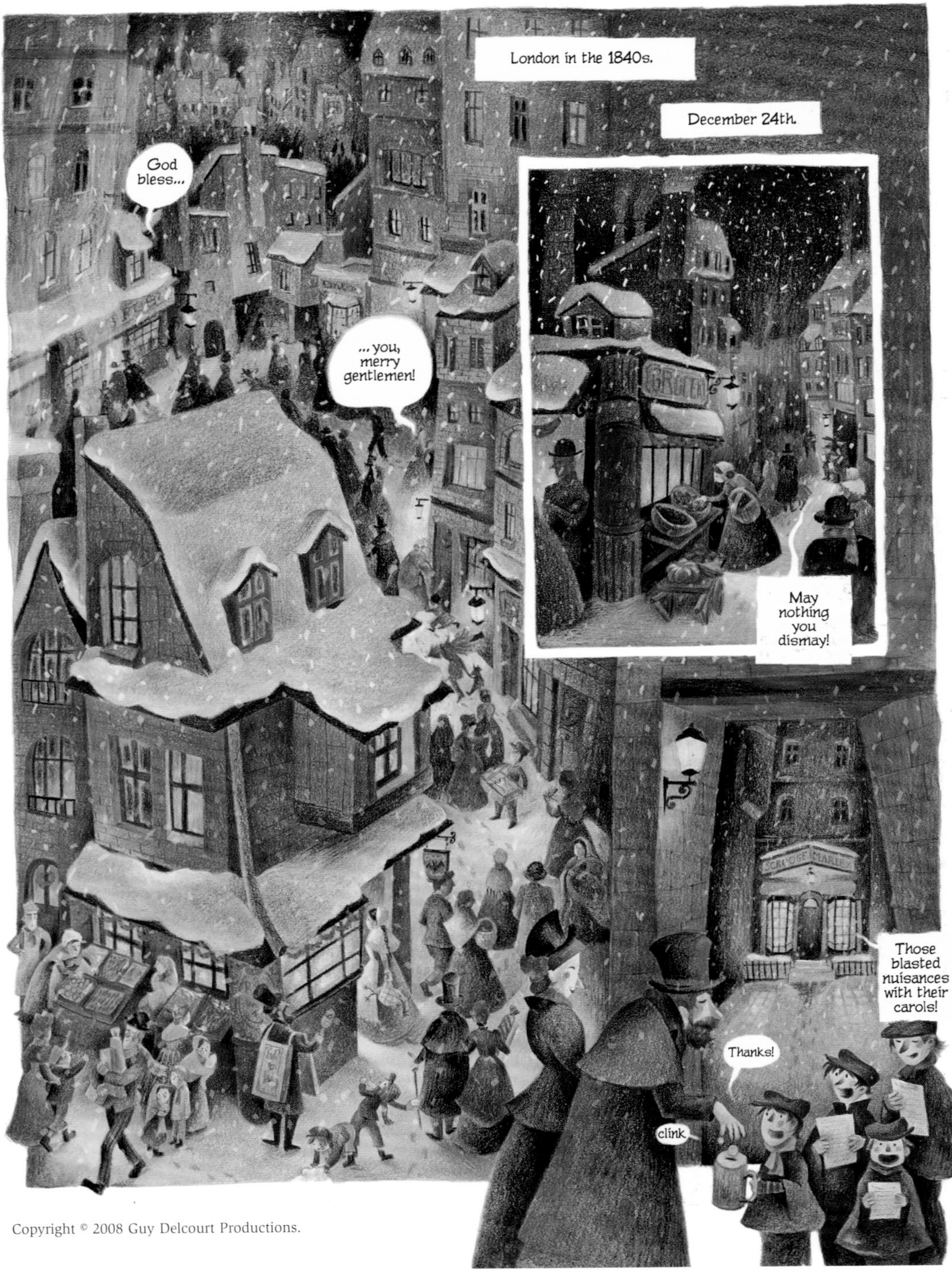
London in the 1840s.
December 24th.
God bless...
...you, merry gentlemen!
GROCER
May nothing you dismay!
SCROOGE MARLEY
Those blasted nuisances with their carols!
Thanks!
clink

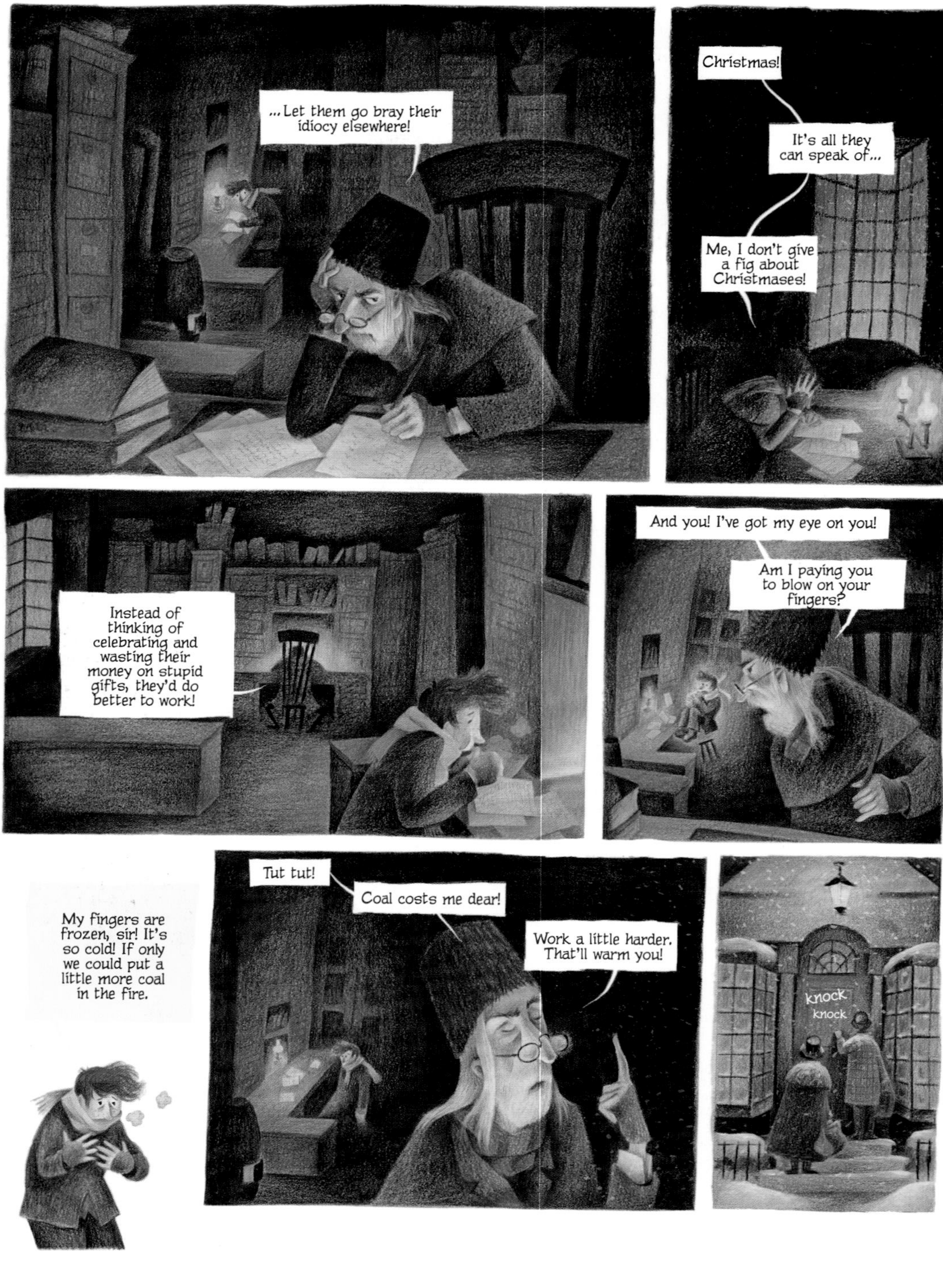
...Let them go bray their idiocy elsewhere!
Christmas!
It's all they can speak of...
Me, I don't give a fig about Christmases!
Instead of thinking of celebrating and wasting their money on stupid gifts, they'd do better to work!
And you! I've got my eye on you!
Am I paying you to blow on your fingers?
My fingers are frozen, sir! It's so cold! If only we could put a little more coal in the fire.
Tut tut!
Coal costs me dear!
Work a little harder. That'll warm you!
knock
knock

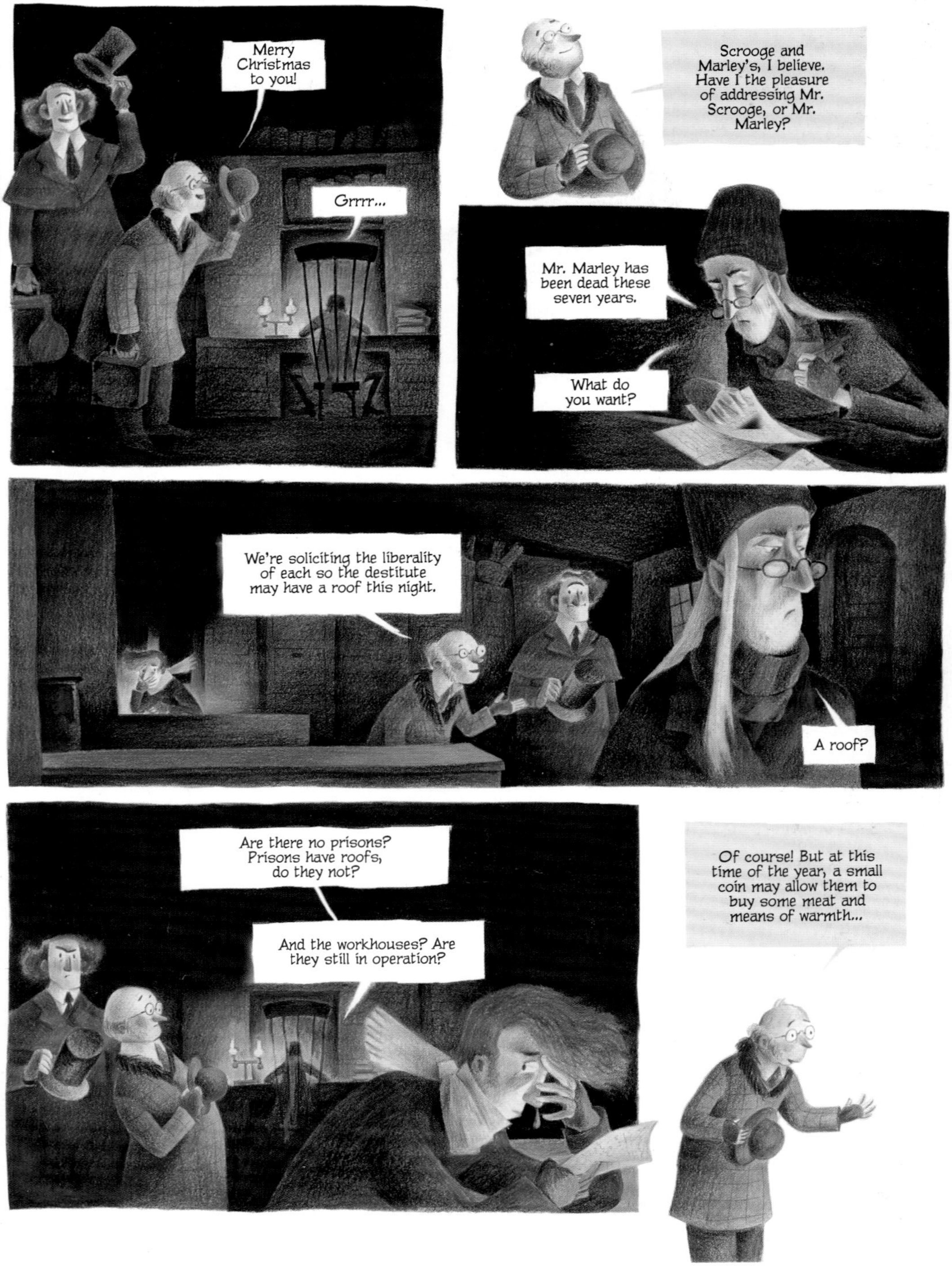
Merry Christmas to you!
Grrrr...
Scrooge and Marley's, I believe. Have I the pleasure of addressing Mr. Scrooge, or Mr. Marley?
Mr. Marley has been dead these seven years.
What do you want?
We're soliciting the liberality of each so the destitute may have a roof this night.
A roof?
Are there no prisons? Prisons have roofs, do they not?
And the workhouses? Are they still in operation?
Of course! But at this time of the year, a small coin may allow them to buy some meat and means of warmth...

What shall I put you down for?
Nothing!
Your wretches have but what they deserve!
And if our establishments don't suit them, if they'd rather die, they had better do it and decrease the surplus population!
Come, Mr. Williams, I see it's useless to pursue our point!
Useless, indeed.
Merry Christmas, sir.